THE HEDGESTONE HERESY

A Novel

ANTHONY RUSSO

Word Art Publishing
9350 Wilshire Blvd
Suite 203, Beverly Hills, CA 90212
www.wordartpublishing.com
Phone: 1 (888) 614 - 1370

Published by Word Art Publishing

ISBN: Paperback   978-1-955070-53-9
       Hardback   978-1-955070-55-3
       Ebook   978-1-955070-54-6

"Our call…is to spiritualise the senses rather than sensualise the spirit".

—*Fredrick Robertson August 4, 1850*

CONTENTS

CHAPTER 1

A DISPLACEMENT
OF THE HEART

Jane stood in the midst of the music. All around her, hands and voices were lifted in earnest worship. The young musicians plied their skills and filled the auditorium with pleasant and soothing notes, each one carrying tingling emotions. The large video screens around the auditorium emblazoned the lyrics over earth images, inviting all to contribute their voices.

But Jane felt strangely disconnected. As if she was invisible, an intruder into the joy of others, not permitted to partake. And perhaps, in part, by her own volition. Although she mouthed the words on the screens around her, they seemed to fall to the ground in front of her, weakened by the heaviness of her own heart. It was as if she was surrounded by a thick veil of suffocating suppression.

Different – is what Jane felt. She felt different, overtaken by something unusual and unfamiliar. Broken in fellowship with those around her, distracted by something beyond her, unsure and unknowing. And Jane was determined to find out why.

Jane was unique in so many ways. A corporate lawyer with one of Sydney's top tier firms. No one was quite sure if it was her natural and quiet beauty or the sharpness of her intellect that drove her rapid acceleration through the trenches and up the ranks of the commercial hierarchy. Whatever the reason, at 29, Jane commanded enormous respect from her peers and the senior partners who kept a watchful eye – and full attention – on her progress. And not without reason. Jane's clients rarely queried her billings and only reluctantly allowed other operatives to work on their account.

Daughter of Christian missionaries to Maputo, Mozambique, her compassion for others and empathy with their needs was authentic and had taken deep root in her character. It was this paradox that made Jane unique. Critically astute in the assessment of the facts, while at the same time, compassionately sensitive to the human players in the story. It was this that produced the truth in tension that caused her to grow strong and straight, like a tree, staked and tied from opposite directions. Ruthless in pursuit of the facts, unemotive and concise in her judgment, willing to expunge all that stood in her way. Yet, seemingly in total contrast to this, she was also creative and sincerely dedicated to the little people in her life: From Suzy, her PA, to the doorman of her apartment building, Jane meticulously memorised everyone's names and needs. At every greeting, she was amazingly able to recall their last conversation and inquire as to the progress of a problem or trouble. Jane cared. And those that knew Jane counted their association a privilege and a personal treasure.

This authentic concern of Jane's was not forced but had deep roots reaching back into her childhood days. In her early and formative years, she had often assisted her father in distributing clothes to children in AIDS orphanages; and medical supplies, to clinics. She remembers her father driving home in the hot African late afternoons, red dust trailing behind them, and suddenly being overcome by a sober and solemn quietness, as he gazed into the tropical sun setting before them, tears welling up in his eyes.

"What's the matter, Dad?" she would ask.

He would quietly respond, "Let's pray Jane," before reaching out and holding her hand. "These people have broken hope," he would say, "unless the power of God's love can reach into their hearts".

Then one by one, they brought the names of those they visited that day before their Lord in earnest and heartfelt intensity.

Jane watched the dedication of her parents with admiration - their labour of love for their mission as they supported each other throughout every trial and disappointment, victory and celebration, providing such a richness of environment for her and her brother Paul that they wanted for nothing.

That's why her world stopped spinning when, with tearful eyes, her father's assistant sat her and her brother down one late evening and told them their parents would not be coming home from their supplies trip to Nelspruit, having been shot dead - murdered by hijackers soon after crossing the South African border.

Jane looked at the plates on the dining table that had just been set, knowing now that they would never be filled, along with the pot of pasta on the stove that would never be served. She felt her heart empty of all the goodness that had been laid up for so many years. Her speech was gone. She searched for words, but none came. She tasted her tears as they ran down her face. She looked for young Paul, who had run out of the house, and was now on his knees, screaming a single word like a chant that was attempting to defy and challenge a new reality, "No! No! No!"

Now in the midst of a church service 15 years later, her father's original home church and the place where he had dedicated much of his life before Africa, she felt a familiar and frightening sense of both abandonment and danger. Something was wrong.

Chapter 2

A Disruption in the Ranks

The Monday morning leaders' review meeting at the Global Outreach Fellowship headquarters was just like all those before them, with a set agenda that was to be executed with military rigor. GOF Executive, Pastor Arthur Hedgestone, moved quickly to establish his authority over proceedings. He rebuked those departmental heads that gave a report not to his liking. He elevated those that praised his weekend messages and commented on how moved they were. The youth leader with a request for consideration to purchase a new BBQ was shut down with a quick and curt, "Take an offering up from your team."

"Teach them how to give," Hedgestone barked.

Arthur Hedgestone indulged himself in the satisfaction of always being in control. This was where he loved to be – his favourite feeling, his comfortable place, his best friend. The mornings' meetings had gone well. Receipts were up, rebels were silenced; his assistants, compliant. Control was cocaine for his soul. No immediate threats appeared to be on the horizon. Unfortunately for Arthur, all of that self-satisfaction was about to end as his cell phone rang out to his favourite chorus: 'He is Lord.'

"Hello," his voice boomed with a distinctive Mr Ed slur.

"Pastor, we have a situation here in Phoenix," said the voice with an overemphasised seriousness.

"Go on," said Hedgestone enquiringly.

"Ron Bones sang songs at this evening's service that were not from your certified songbook. I got the call from a very concerned young disciple who also said that Bones spent longer in praise than normal."

Hedgestone thanked the informant with a definite and curt, "Thank you, brother," giving the caller no opportunity to draw him into a discussion or sense the seriousness in his voice. Mental notes were made, and a final instruction was issued: "Keep me informed," he said.

Again, the following morning, Hedgestone's sense of security was challenged. Although it was four-thirty am, the phone only rang twice before Hedgestone's hand was on it. He ran his fellowship of churches like a military general. Honouring the importance of intelligence and communication was not lost on him.

"Hello?" he almost demanded.

"Pastor Hedgestone?" The Australian accent was immediately recognisable. Fat, failed and unfruitful was how Hedgestone had labelled this man. Although he despised the man on the other end of the phone, he was all ears when it came to news from Down Under, given their constant jibing and challenging of his authority in recent years. The significant value of the property assets that had accrued there over the years had also not gone unnoticed by him.

"Pastor Hedgestone, its Curly Walker from Sydney. I hope I haven't rung you at the wrong time?"

'You idiot,' thought Hedgestone, 'you can't even tell the time.'

Out loud he said, "Oh, Curly, how's your family? Well?"

Hedgestone greased Curly with all the lubrication required for him to feel comfortable enough to be forthcoming with his information on the local Sydney scene.

"All good, thank you, Pastor," Walker replied. "I wonder if I can discuss some concerns I have from our recent Shepherds' seminar?"

"Go on," said Hedgestone, sensing something useful was about to come forth. Hedgestone's radar was on and honing in. His investment in Walker's airfares and expenses for him to attend the recent US conference in LA were starting to pay off.

"Pastor, I felt that Gavin Hickery's leadership messages were inappriate and undermining of your authority. He spoke about the need to enlarge our vision and embrace all that God is doing on the earth and not just focus on our fellowship of churches."

Walker knew what Hedgestone wanted to hear: 'Nobody is doing what we're doing,' was the oft-repeated mantra. "I told him no one was doing what we are doing, that we had a special and clear call, a master blueprint, a unique anointing in the last days. But he insisted that God is bigger than just our vision."

"Well, thank you, brother, for letting me know your concerns," said Hedgestone. "I will bring you all before the Lord in prayer for direction," he said, speaking with all the fairy floss sweetness of a Christmas elf, and the veiled threatening danger of a wolf's fangs.

Hedgestone needed no encouragement to suspect a conspiracy at work to loosen his vice-like grip on leadership, authority and of course, cash at bank. Just when he thought his Fellowship was tightly bolted! Something was undoubtedly threatening to unravel all his hard work, and he intended to tighten or replace every loose screw he could find in his machine of 900 churches in 32 countries to prevent that from occurring.

Although they were 12,000 kilometres apart and neither of them knew it, a convergent force beyond either of their comprehension was about to bring Hedgestone and Jane into an arena of conflict that would challenge the depths of all their skills and perseverance. There would only be one winner.

CHAPTER 3

A MYSTERIOUS LETTER

It was Monday, and Jane had just begun to work through the latest round of contract amendments leftover from Friday night. However, she could not escape the unsettling experience from yesterday's Sunday service.

'What was that I felt?' she questioned herself. 'Like I was gazing hopelessly into the same face of the 2002 drama.'

'Am I too touchy-feely?" she cross-examined herself.

'Is my imagination in overdrive?'

'How could I feel such a sense of dread in what was supposed to be a sanctuary for spiritual replenishment,' she reasoned.

Jane's strength of mind quickly vanquished these circling doubts. She knew what she felt. And what she felt was so incredibly strong. A sense of alienation and an agenda of deception from those she had trusted most of her life began to grow within her. She felt both unclean at admitting these feelings but at the same time, she felt as if someone had shown her the innermost secrets of a man's heart.

"Wow, you are looking far too deep for a Monday!" said her young PA, Suzy, interrupting her thoughts.

"Oh, it's nothing," said Jane disarming her help from any further inquisition.

"Hmm, I'm not so sure," said Suzy. "Anyway, Tommy rang and wants to catch up with you for lunch."

Now she had Jane's attention.

'That is exactly what I need,' Jane thought silently, not wanting Suzy to sense her delight at what a great idea that would be right now. "Ask him to meet me at one pm at the Black Cat Café," requested Jane with well-masked disinterest.

Lunch. That's what she needed. Lunch with a trusted friend. Tommy was that go-to guy for such concerns as the last 24 hours. On so many issues, they lived inside each other's heads. While some men and colleagues often sought conversation as a ruse for cultivating romantic interest, she trusted that this was not Tommy's primary motivation. Although he was strikingly handsome in a Portuguese, Latino sort of way, Jane had always felt comfortable enough to share anything with Tommy. Their paths had criss-crossed since pre-school days in Africa. They had kept in contact through their teenage years and supported each other during tertiary studies as both pursued professional legal careers. Then four years ago, she was thrilled when Tommy had contacted her to support his sponsorship application for migration to Australia.

Jane spotted Tommy at their favourite table, deeply immersed in his cell phone screen. She smiled to herself, ready to find some relief and comfort in his possible counsel.

"Hey, why so long?" she jabbed Tommy, taking him by surprise.

"Jane!" Tommy he rose from his seat and greeted Jane with a warm embrace.

"Well, stranger, mainly because you seem to be off-the-grid lately, old girl," Tommy defended. But he didn't need to.

"Yeah, sorry, been buried with work," retorted Jane.

"Gosh, you are looking good, Tommy!" said Jane.

"Well, that's the benefit of working with not-for-profits rather than commercial blue chips," Tommy responded. "I can go home with the satisfaction of a day's work well done and leave it at the office."

"Yes, and I go home and start the second shift at nine pm after a microwaved version of food," complained Jane.

"Let's order."

Chitchat and reminiscing over their Africa days dominated the conversation as they worked through a shared plate of pesto gnocchi and a chardonnay. Finally, Jane felt comfortably relaxed enough to share her burden with Tommy.

"Tommy, something has really been troubling me over the weekend, and I don't know how to describe it other than an impending shadow of gloom and doom," she began.

"What do you mean?" enquired Tommy with concern.

"I've got to get back to the office but can we catch up on Friday night? My shout, Degas is exhibiting at the Arts Centre, and I don't want to miss it. Let's go together and then grab something to eat."

"OK, sure," accepted Tommy.

"Thanks for the meal, Tommy. I will see you on Friday, but I have to rush back now," said Jane as she picked up the tab and headed for the door.

Back at the office, Jane began to feel some relief from having shared her burden with Tommy. That was until she worked through the mail on her desk and noticed an unmarked envelope, sealed and marked for her attention. She opened it with trepidation and began to read the letter, handwritten in poor and broken English.

Dear Ms Jane,

It has been many, many years since we have spoken and maybe you are not remembering me. My name is Sipho, and I was your father's assistant in his work in Maputo. It was such a delight watching you and your younger brother growing up all those years ago. Many beautiful memories I have. I am sorry, sorry it has taken so long for me to write to you on this matter, but as the years have passed, I have been increasingly challenged to share several things with you concerning the death of your parents, which as you know was a source of great grief and shock to us all. It has taken me some time to find you as well. I don't want to write everything down here. Can you please call me and I can explain? My number is on the card enclosed. Please, I look forward to hearing your voice again.

Yours sincerely,
Sipho Mbane

Jane instantly remembered Sipho! His friendly face emerged in her mind's eye on the page as she read his letter. She was carried back to a multitude of memories and colourful cameos of her father and Sipho working together on the mission.

Now she knew that what she felt was no accident. Her heart raced. Her ability to concentrate on work was fading, while her sense of urgency and need to hear Sipho's voice only grew until it become overwhelming. She found his card in the envelope and headed home.

"I will see you tomorrow, Suzy. I've got a statement to prep for filing tomorrow and will work from home," Jane said, excusing herself.

"But you haven't spilled anything on the charming and still lonely Tommy!" begged Suzy. "Another time Suzy," Jane deflected and kept walking.

Jane reached for the phone as soon as she got in the door. She fumbled for the card and began dialling the numbers. She knew it was still very early in Maputo, but she could not delay. Again, Jane felt her heart race as she heard the call begin to ring.

"Allo?" came the deep African voice from afar.

"Sipho! Is that you?" cried Jane with elation. "It's Jane Johnson, from Sydney Australia. I got your letter. How are you? It's been so many years, but I've never forgotten you," she said with all the fullness of sincerity for which she was known by her peers.

"Yes, it is me, Ms Jane. I am so glad to hear your voice again," said Sipho. "I have many things to tell you, and I am so sorry it has taken me this long, but my health has been leaving me and I am very much needing to speak with you."

She listened intensely to every word coming from Sipho over the next hour. The gentleness and rhythm of his voice were not able to soften the devasting content of his words, though. Tears began to roll down Jane's face uncontrollably.

At times, the emotion reached down deep into her soul, and she had to cover her mouth, not wanting to distract Sipho from his story with her heart-wrenching sobs. It was five pm before she ended the call, agreeing they must speak again soon. This was too much. Jane was overwhelmingly distressed and utterly unprepared to deal with what Sipho had shared.

Chapter 4

Renewed Friendships

Jane loved art – any art! She always found it intriguing how people like herself could visit a gallery and come away inspired or moved by all of the ideas and thoughts presented by the artist. The Edgar Degas *Dancers* exhibition was just such an opportunity, even though she knew his personal story to be one of darkness and depression for much of his life.

While Jane waited for Tommy to turn up, her thoughts drifted to the paradox of how artistic inspiration came not just from within the artist themselves, but from observing people such as herself. All the dimensions of an obscure humanity – from the attitudes and poses of faceless ballerinas, to their movements, in Degas's case, along with their interactions – these observations were replayed back to society via the media of paint, words and music. The artist went to the people to get their raw material and then turned these ideas and thoughts into a mirror that reflected their impressions back to their subjects. 'We pay an entrance fee just to see what we look like,' Jane often mused to herself.

So too, she thought, had Jesus come and observed humankind in all of their sins, trouble and pain, and then produced the cross, a symbol that played this drama back to all of us; as if to say: this is what love and sin look like. A work of art and sacrifice, with himself as the medium of communication. Grace made flesh, screaming for our attention and consideration. What a picture that cross was! What a testimony for all of eternity! Yes, other artists could interpret the event in marble or paint, but Jesus was the event! His life was the work of art. Beautiful as it was haunting; convincing, as it was gracious and accepting. Both horror and love, amidst blood, nails and thorns. Nakedness without shame, a life surrendered but still victorious.

Jane's thoughts advanced. All of our lives could be a work of art, she pondered. We are all artists. Our lives are a poem. We are His workmanship. We can all live a life that absorbs the pain, and play back the answers, hopes and fulfilment found in His example. Wow! The whole world could be a gallery of God's grace!

Jane's grand attempts to understand spiritual peace and global reconciliation were suddenly interrupted by Tommy's comforting voice. "Jane, there you are! Shall we go in?"

"Let's," said Jane.

They moved quickly from room to room, contemplating the progression of images before them. Flashes of colour from the delicately rendered dresses of the dancers stood out against the cold and dark shadows of disciplined training dance studio halls. Jane and Tommy explored why the dancer's faces were so obscure and without definition or any hint of happiness, almost torturous in their expressions.

"Is it because that is who Degas was?" suggested Jane. "Was he as miserable as some of his ballerinas look?"

"Maybe," responded Tommy. "Maybe as an artist, you can never reach beyond who you are as a person. Yes, the technical skill is there, but any heartfelt intent towards something wholesome, something desirable or beautiful is absent," observed Tommy. "That's why we need to work on who we are, so we can present what one might call 'good art.' Out of the abundance of the heart, or deficiency therein, the eye sees and the hand paints."

"Remarkable!" Jane responded. "You never cease to amaze me at how you can sum up something so complex in less than 60 seconds!"

"Anyway, enough deep and meaningfulness. Hungry? My shout for the poor, pro bono, social lawyer."

Jane and Tommy made their way to the Treble Clef, a favourite of Jane's for its subdued ambience, soft lighting and delicate, small portion designed menu. They found a table for two in a quiet corner and indulged in some desserts and strong, long macchiatos.

"OK, so let's get down to it, Jane. What's been going on with you?" Tommy said with a level of assertiveness that surprised Jane. You call me and get me all concerned, but what is this all about?"

"Tommy, you know I'm a facts and figures kind of girl, right? You know I'm all about hardcore analysis and like to drill down to the detail under the data?"

"OK," conceded Tommy.

"Well, that's why I'm totally out of my depth here. First, I get all of these weird sensations of alienation in church last Sunday, like I don't belong there, and this is all fake, smoke and mirrors - packaged truth with deception inside. Like I'm being told to run for my life."

"Go on," said Tommy, looking intensely into those large beautiful eyes that he had learned to admire so many years ago as kids growing up in Africa.

"Then after our coffee this week, I get back to the office and there on my desk was a letter from Sipho Mbane! You remember Sipho, right?"

"Yes, of course," acknowledged Tommy. Your father's right-hand man in Maputo. So thankful was he for your fathers' friendship to his family that he became the link between your dad and the local community in Maputo."

"Yep, that's him. So, his letter asks me to call him ASAP. So, I go home that afternoon, and he tells me that the timing and manner of Mum and Dad's death seemed very suspicious to him. He says Dad had major, significant challenges from the church leadership in the US – apparently, they had threatened to remove him from his post, claiming that they no longer 'endorsed his ministry,'" said Jane, beginning to shake and become increasingly emotional with as she spoke.

"But that's crazy!" protested Tom. "Your dad's church was a beacon in that whole southern African region. Such rapid growth, a quality congregation that was financially self-supporting. And all of those local community support ministries he launched – it was amazing!"

"I know. That's why I find it all so strange… But Sipho says Dad was pressed into handing his church over to the Fellowship leadership, that they wanted to remove him and put in someone else that was more 'loyal and aligned' to old Hedgestone in the USA. He says Mum and Dad refused to leave, that they had made Africa their home, and they felt no inclination to move on at all. He challenged them if it was because of the growth and influence his church now had. They took this as a 'statement of rebellion.'"

Jane was beginning to break down. Those large blue eyes were now welling up with tears.

"I can't believe this," said Tommy. "I always felt Hedgestone was over the top in many ways, but this would be a contradiction of all of his doctrines on the power and purpose of a local church. He always said he respected local church governance and would not meddle or interfere in their affairs."

Jane reached for Tommy's hands and gripped them tightly, as if she needed to hold onto something solid in order to finish her story. "Sipho says Hedgestone was somehow involved in the carjacking and shooting! Tell me this can't be true? Tell me Sipho has got it wrong!"

She continued before he could respond. "But he says he recently found some of Dad's old files and documents, and met with several people that confirmed his worst fears."

The tears began to roll. Jane dropped her head and tried to regain her self-control. "My parents murdered by the church leadership they served with all the life that was in them?" entreated Jane, not sure if she was asking a question or making a statement.

Tommy felt his heart race and slumped back into his chair, gobsmacked at Jane's story. Two thoughts flashed through his head at the same time. Firstly, the shock and awe of what he had just heard, and secondly, in an untimed infinite instance of revelation, like seeing a new colour for the first time, he felt Jane's pain deep within his own soul, and realised just how deeply he felt for this girl who sat across from him, while she dissolved into a shaking, weeping mess.

After a while, Jane pulled herself together with the help of a tissue from Tommy.

"I don't know what to do next, Tommy," she said. "Do I really want to find out or do I want to pretend none of this happened?"

Tommy found himself moving from shock to a sense of righteous anger. This was wrong and needed to be made right. "There is only one thing to do," Tommy responded with unexpected authority. "We are going to Africa. Anything else would be a dishonour to your parents and their ministry, and I, for one, am not going to let that happen."

Chapter 5

A Wolf in The Moonlight

Hedgestone slept alone. His wife, Beatrice, had long since lost patience with his snoring. Too many lost nights of sleep interrupted by the raucous sound of sawing timber saw her take up nightly residence in one of the kid's old bedrooms. But snoring was not Hedgestone's main problem. It was the nightmares, and one recurring, terrifying sequence kept replaying with increasing frequency these days.

Hedgestone saw himself as a shepherd of sheep high up in the mountains of a Scottish wilderness. Proudly he walked through the valleys and peaks, herding and leading and admiring his flocks. And counting, always counting them. He was sure someone was stealing his sheep. Not only that, he felt sure that there was a wild beast at large that was attacking the flock.

Tonight was one such night. As he reached REM sleep, Hedgestone began to toss from side to side. In the midst of his sheep inspection, his teeth began to grind. As he was scrutinising his sheep, he was sure he was a few down. Then he saw the trail of blood. He began to sweat as he followed the path of blood to the grisly discovery of a carcass. The head was nearly severed, and the guts spewed forth on the ground with an awful stench.

"Another one!" Hedgestone angrily declared. "Not another one!" There was no sorrow for the sheep. It was the future loss of productivity and one less sheep to fleece that so angered him. "I'm gonna get you!" he screamed to the jagged rocks, as if they were the beastly culprit. He dreamed on in living colour.

"Tonight!" he declared, as he knew a full moon was rising. "I'm gonna catch that murderous, thieving monster tonight." He waited up late in the evening. Then with the full moon providing a clear opportunity for navigation, he armed himself with his sharpest and longest dagger, and set off into the hills. Jumping from rock to rock, he worked his way through his fields. Finally, he saw something heading towards one particular flock. He moved quickly to close the gap between the shadowy figure and himself. Finally, he was in reach.

He climbed the rock in front of him to get a height advantage. With his footing anchored in place, he leapt onto the monster under cover of full darkness, just as the clouds floated across the moon. He complimented himself on his strategy as he connected with the beast and wrestled him to the ground. The two figures jostled for position, rolling down the side of the hill. Finally, with the monster beneath him, he lifted his dagger high above his head and held his enemy by the throat. "I've got you now!" claimed Hedgestone victoriously.

Then, just as he was about to thrust the dagger into the bared throat beneath him, the moon broke through the clouds and shone onto the face of his suspected enemy. Hedgestone screamed, violently! The knife dropped from his clenched fist. He looked directly into the face of his captive. The face was that of himself.[1]

His scream broke the silence as Hedgestone woke up and sat on the side of his bed, grasping for a sense of reality. Slowly, he caught his breath, calmed himself before collapsing back onto his pillow. Peering at the ceiling, he tried to make sense of it all. But his pride would not allow understanding to reach his mind, the notion that he was the murderer of his own flock. He reached for his Bible to calm his thoughts. Randomly he opened it and began to read the first passage on the page. His heart suddenly skipped a beat as he read the words of an Old Testament Prophet, Nathan, who, with a bony finger pointed to King David, before saying, "Thou art the man!"

---

[1] From a Poem, by Hall Caine, T & T Clark, The Waverley Book Company Ltd

CHAPTER 6

THE REAL JESUS

Jane was both thankful and surprised at Tommy taking the lead in her troubled circumstances. While she was secretly looking for sympathy from Tommy, she did not expect his total empathy or decision to launch himself into the midst of her troubles and stand right alongside her. She had decided long ago that she would never return to Africa. The emotional trauma was just too much. She had not been back in fourteen years.

It was Africa that broke her world in two. It was Africa, she thought, that had taken her parents away from her, amidst their labour and sacrifice. And now it was Africa that was again threatening to disrupt the calm and ordered world she had built for herself, by herself, over many years of working part-time jobs to get through university, followed by late nights and seven-day working weeks.

This is what she wrestled and struggled with for the longest time. 'And God, where were you?' Jane often thought. What about all of the promises they grew up with? Promises her parents had built their lives and decisions upon. Expectations like His protection and assurance and favour and blessing. How could you make a mockery of all of that?

It was many years before Jane was even willing to go anywhere near a church. The only reason she ever rebuilt any relationship with God was not because of any church organisation but because she could not deny the life and death of Jesus, who he was and what he died for, and she had seen all of that genuinely reflected in the lives her parents had lived.

Turning to the gospel pages through those shadowy years, alone in Australia, trying to reconnect with her faith and rebuild her life, again and again, Jane found the characters and cameos in the writings of Luke and John to be the only thing that made sense to her world. Step by step, she began to retrace the footprints of when she had walked with her parents and the Lord. So many Christ cameos, of Jesus speaking into the life of women, that completely fascinated her. Not structured theology, not religious poetry, but real people, coming face to face with the Man of their moment.

To the woman at the well, playing charades around a history of five husbands, five broken and failed relationships, five times nothing was still nothing. He says drink of the water that He gives and you will never thirst, that you will access a spring of 'everlasting life.' His promise of quenching thirst, a desire, a longing for love and affection that nothing else she tried ever could.

To the woman 'caught' in adultery, who had been dragged through the streets half-naked to a gathering crowd who had collected rocks along the way, and been thrown before Jesus for judgement. In less than 60 seconds, in a flash of nuclear conviction, judgement is turned away, and she hears life-changing words, 'Neither do I condemn you, go and sin no more.' She hears the rocks, previously aimed for her head, thud into the ground. She dares not look up but can see through her tears and tangled hair around her face, that the feet of those judging her begin to turn and walk away, miraculously confronted with their failures and therein disqualified from judging others.

To the centurion whose daughter had 'died,' only to discover that faith and confidence in the spoken word of Jesus, the Man could restore the love of his life to his family's arms.

To Mary and Martha, friends of Jesus, sisters distressed by the death of their brother Lazarus, and questioning why He delayed in coming when Lazarus fell ill, she found Jesus words of life, direction, hope and restoration as thoroughly refreshing as a well in a harsh desert. 'I AM the resurrection and the life.'

Jane got it. Without him, there was no life. She could stay in the cold dark tomb with her Lazarus, the dark shroud of death in Africa, or respond to his invitation to join the living. She could tear off the tight death robes that had so constrained and constricted her life and heart, and move into the light and warmth of a new day, out of the depth of a cold, dark tomb. It was up to her. She could hear His words and take life for all it promised. Jane believed.

She drank long and often at this well, meditated and rotated and agitated the words and responses of Jesus. Faith grew. Jane saw herself as another feminine face in the crowd, and Jesus had looked straight into her soul and called her out. She was able to peg and picture and frame and understand the commitment of her parent's life choices. This truth was worth it. It was this that moved her to study law. Hunger for truth became Jane's justifying refuge, purpose and cause.

She challenged herself to move on. The life-giving words of Jesus took root in her own heart. She loved who He was. He made sense. As she saw this life navigating magneto within her heart and this precious jewel of relationship encompassing her soul, Jane had decided that she would not do anything that would upset or challenge or threaten the life-giving residence that Jesus had now taken up within her. Old habits and self-pitying thought journeys gave way to decisive new hopes and dreams. Desires changed, life was new, and Jane could move forward.

Now, with Tommy's support, she knew she had to go back. Tommy was right. He didn't say it, but this was not God's fault - this was not meant to happen. Her parent's work was not over. Their story was not finished. Jane now felt just as confident that it was time for her to play her part, as Jesus had played His role many years ago. This sense of purpose began to rise within her. Fear gave way to determination. She didn't believe in accidents - not that of her parent's tragedy 14 years ago – and not what she'd felt in that Sunday service only a week ago.

Chapter 7

A Journey into The Past

Jane's request for a week's special leave at short notice was approved, although she had to throw in a promise to stay online for urgent emails. Tommy was able to convince his senior partner that there was an overarching social justice connection to the trip. Jane got Suzy to make the flight and accommodation bookings for her and Tommy – not a bright move, on reflection, as Suzy was overly insistent that the request for separate rooms was a deliberate red herring.

It was quietly surreal when Tommy arrived at Jane's apartment at five-thirty am for the airport pickup with light rain falling on that cold July morning. The events of the last few days had moved quickly, and the possibilities confronting him were all so dramatic. As Tommy drove to Jane's that morning, he peered through the wet windscreen with only the squeaky wipers challenging his thoughts.

His mind began to play out all the possible scenarios. 'OK, so let's say old Sipho is right and that Jane's parents were murdered not by random hijackers but in a deliberate and well planned, organised hit. More, that this was no coincidence and that the church leadership disputes leading up to that sad day implicated many current men still in leadership with possible involvement, including the renowned Pastor Arthur Hedgestone, the main in charge for the last 35 years of the Global Outreach Fellowship organisation. Then what? Where do we go with that?'

'Evidence,' thought Tommy. 'That's the disciplined approach. Let's get on the trail and get the proof – then we can think about what we do with it. Let's not get too far ahead of ourselves without some facts behind us to set the direction and the pace of momentum.'

And what was it that he felt for Jane that night? He thought he had put Jane out of any romantic contentions years ago but after seeing her that night in all of her desperation and sheer helplessness, he knew for a fact that he cared too much, that her wellbeing was an absolute imperative for him. 'She mustn't know,' he thought. 'At least not right now…'

But since that night, Jane was in his thoughts continually. From childhood memories of growing up together, to later high school secrets shared and teenage confidences committed, they both knew each other better than perhaps they even admitted to themselves. They reconnected for the first time a few years ago after they had both taken separate journeys. Tommy thought it a little corny to think anything else of their friendship. He also felt that Jane had perhaps grown a fraction more conceited in her professional success, although he now acknowledged that was probably his insecurity at the lack of progress in his.

Anyway, one thing he knew for sure. He increasingly wanted to spend time in Jane's presence, to observe and absorb the smallest details of who Jane was, and the person she had become. He texted her when he was downstairs and peered through the rain, watching for her delicate frame through the decorative obscure glass doors of her apartment foyer. Tommy smiled as he saw Jane coming towards him. He walked back to the car, popped the boot and took her bag while Jane jumped in the car.

"This all seems so surreal," said Jane through a sleepy yawn.

"I know what you mean. I feel the same thing," replied Tommy. "But I think we are meant to be doing this."

"I know what you mean there," replied Jane, borrowing Tommy's line. "I always swore that I would never go back, but now I feel this sense of urgency to catch up with Sipho and get to the bottom of this. Sipho said he had some people he wanted us to meet. I want to know what happened all those years ago."

"And you will," affirmed Tommy. "Once and for all. I want you to know I am with you on this. Part of me is buried there as well, you know. I'll never forget all those days with your Mum and Dad, and you and Paul, how you'd come over to my parents' house, and chat and laugh and encourage us with such a genuine and warm friendship that took all of the harshness and difficulty out of those tough days in Maputo. I would often lie in bed after you guys had gone home, and listen to my parents talk together about how thankful they were to know your mum and dad."

"I do remember those times," said Jane, wistfully. "And your dad, trying to teach my parents Portuguese – so funny! Australians, trying to pronounce those difficult words and phrases." 'Obrigado,' was about all my dad could manage. Luckily, we had you guys to help us with the translations of all his teaching notes."

Jane and Tommy's reminiscing was interrupted by the approaching airport parking gate. Tom fumbled for a credit card to access the car park. They quickly found a spot and boarded the bus to the terminal. Fortunately, given the early hour, security and check-in queues were moving swiftly. They made their way through passport control and to the gate. Thirty-five minutes later, they were finding their space on the plane.

"Did you tell Sipho *we* are coming?" asked Tommy as he took Jane's carry-on without asking and found a space for it in the overhead locker.

"Sure did. He is going to meet us at the airport," Jane answered firmly, a little disturbed that Tommy would ask such a question.

They nestled into their seats and drifted into travel zombie mode while moving through take-off preliminaries. The early morning flight time began to creep up on both of them, and they nodded off, only to be interrupted by the captain's welcome 30 minutes later.

Jane broke the silence as they both stirred from their nap time. "So, are you still attending a church in Sydney?"

"Me? Nope, I've just found it necessary to move on over the last few years," replied Tommy.

"So, what does that mean?" pressed Jane.

"What it means," began Tommy, without wanting to sound overly defensive, "is that I've decided that the modern western evangelical church is not for me. Everything is so 'sloganised' and corporatised. People aren't encouraged to think and grow any more. The emphasis is on joining 'teams' and 'following the leader.' The very last time I was in church, I had to walk out on some idiot preaching on 'Yes Culture.' *Just say yes! Don't think about it! Let yes be your first response to anything you are asked to do.'* Shocking. I found it all so slick, artificial, forced and without authenticity. It's not what we were birthed into in your dad's day and his personal, authentic approach to ministry. Now we have to put up with 'digital discipleship' and Skype video conferencing messages from control central. Give me a bucket so I can throw up. It's all so staged and rehearsed and managed - nothing spiritual in it. And the messages! Just fairy floss, band-aids and happy juice. Nothing more than huff, puff, bluff and fluff. I feel incredibly alienated and manipulated."

Tommy needed to draw breath, but not for long. "And what is it with this 'campus' thing? We don't have a local church any more with a local leader and local governance from the membership that meets local community needs. What we have is centralised theocracy and leadership from a head location. And because we are no longer a 'church,' but a rather a 'campus,' we seem to have lost the safety of the *presbeteros* and the *episkopus*, the simplicity of a pastor and an eldership from the body."

Tommy was done.

"Wow, you have thought about this a lot more than I have," said Jane, not realising the door she had opened with a simple question. "Now that you mention it, that sounds just like our church. They recently introduced this thing called 'gather-grow-go.' I mean, what is that? Why do we always need rhymes and slogans, like you say, to motivate people? Sometimes I feel as though they treat us as if we were in kindergarten, looking for conditioned, autocue responsiveness."

"Yeah, well it's not what your dad taught us 15 years ago," said Tommy. "It was alive and living. People had meaningful and helpful relationships with one another."

Tommy reached for his phone. "Read this blog post by a burnt-out, ex youth pastor from one of Sydney's most 'happening' thumping churches. I think he sums it up well:

We, the leaders of the charismatic church, have built on hype, sensation, innovation, programs, personality and charisma. This has produced: shallowness; false movements; novice leaders— gifted but immature and untested; a deficient understanding of God's word; the building of man-centred, rather than kingdom-centred churches and ministries; competition rather than cooperation; humanistic, self-centred Christians who don't understand sacrifice and commitment; Christians without discernment; superstar leaders; a perverted and powerless gospel; prayerless and anaemic Christians; a replacement of the fear of the Lord with the fear of man; and a young generation that is cynical of it all.[2]

"OK, this is getting freaky," confessed Jane. "That sounds so true, even in our church. Do you remember I told you earlier, how I just felt so disconnected and alienated recently? Like I did not belong there? But I couldn't articulate or explain why," said Jane.

"I'm telling you, Jane," continued Tommy, "I feel like the modern church age is coming to an end. There is a mega-change in the wind. People are growing weary of bouncing along with tired formulae, irrelevant messages and preacher egos that leave no room to see who Jesus the Man really is."

Jane pondered Tommy's thoughts. She knew he was right, the more she thought about it. He seemed to be able to articulate and unveil many of the buried feelings and unspoken suspicions that lay deep within her. She was building a new appreciation for Tommy's intellect. He had definitely changed, matured, become stronger in his convictions then the whimsical young man she had known previously. This was going to be an interesting few days, in more ways than one, she thought as she nestled down into selecting a movie. Tommy took the hint when he saw the headphones go on that Jane wanted some personal time.

---

[2] Source Unknown

CHAPTER 8

DARK MEMORIES

The connection through Johannesburg to the local carrier and onto Maputo went reasonably well, as far as African flights go, thought Jane as they boarded the final leg.

The reality of returning to Maputo after so many years was finally dawning on both of them. Firstly, the racial make-up of this flight was unmistakably black, compared to the flight out of Sydney. Then there was the mix of languages, not so much English now amongst her flight companions. Instead, it was an eclectic mix of Portuguese, Swahili, Zulu and Nyanja. Voices were louder, people were larger, and space was limited. Jane watched and remembered as she saw passengers push those red, white and blue-striped acrylic bags into overhead lockers, casting aside anyone else's bags with abandon to make room for their own. One thing she remembered from her years in Africa: Everyone owned a good number of those large multi-purpose bags. Large enough for carrying your shopping home from the market and versatile enough to keep the rain off your head if you got caught walking home in an African summer downpour.

"Well, we should be on schedule for Sipho," said Jane with expectation, as she buckled in. "I have this happy-scared feeling going on inside. I'm sort of excited to walk again in those places that trigger so many good memories of times past, but then scared of reigniting the terrifying feelings of when I lost Mum and Dad, and super scared of what Sipho might have to share with us."

Tommy knew it was the wrong time to speak. He continued to listen intently with his dark eyes, not breaking contact with Jane's blues.

Jane continued, "You know I went through just the darkest time of hatred after the funeral. I so loved my parents. I was 16. I still needed them every day, but every day there was just this terrible loneliness, this frozen silence, this absence of their voices. I felt it was more than I could bear. Mealtimes were the worst. Just Paul and me, looking at each other, often crying tears into our food, grief and sadness robbing us of any appetite. I had no answers for Paul, although I would practice little speeches I had worked out in bed every night that I would try and fit into the next day. Words of encouragement that I'd try and find a place to drop into Paul's emptiness. But nothing I could say would make a dent in that void for him. I watched him drift away from me like a sailboat loosed from its pier. And then as I began to give up on him, I saw the same darkness that crept over Paul begin to try and claim me. And that was when hatred for everything my parents lived and died for entered me like an unwelcome intruder that I refused to ask to leave. I hated all gospel endeavour, churches, everything. I wanted to punch God. I refused even to speak the name of Jesus. I resented every Sunday School song that tried to creep back into my heart, wanting to be sung. I hated all of it. I wanted none of it anymore. I had asked the 'why' questions so many times: 'Why me, why mum and dad, why did we come here, why did they have to feel this sense of obligation to others, why us, why, why, why?' so many times, that I hated the sound of my inner voice." Jane finished softly, almost whispering those last words.

She turned to look at Tommy, only to find those dark Latino eyes filling with tears, even though he tried to blink them away and pretend this wasn't happening. "Oh, I'm so sorry," said Jane. "I didn't mean to dump all that on you."

Tommy still had no words. There was only one thing he could do, and without thinking, he did it. Awkwardly reaching across the armrests of the plane seats, he threw his arms around her in reckless abandon. They sobbed into each other's arms for a moment. "It's

OK, I was there, remember?" said Tommy in an attempt to console Jane.

"Yes, I remember," said Jane as she politely disentangled herself from Tommy's embrace. "But then you left me too…"

"I didn't leave," said Tommy defending himself. "You moved back to Australia, and I didn't know where, and I didn't know how to react, to be honest. It was all just a painful mess."

"Well, that's true, but still, you took a long time to come and find me," said Jane, and for the first time, Tommy got some confirmation that he had, to an extent, remained in her thoughts after all that time. Like a small trophy, he tucked that away into his heart. It crossed his legal mind to suggest that Jane could have equally made an effort to look him up, but he certainly was not looking for an argument at this time.

"Anyway, after all of that, here we are, in a plane, together, about to step back in time and pick things up where we left off, yes? And that is amazing on so many different levels. So, let's take the chance to pick up from where we left off, and find out what happened all those years ago, for both of us," said Tommy.

Jane shrugged in tacit agreement, not sure whether to welcome Tommy's efforts to take the lead in this expedition or resent the challenge to hers. They both nestled back into their seats to seek some comfort and pass the remaining hour of the journey.

CHAPTER 9

OLD ACQUAINTANCES

Sipho had to pinch himself that this moment had finally arrived. Three times that day, he had monitored the flights to make sure there were no delays, and everything was running on time. He had so looked forward to Jane's arrival since that phone call a few days ago. Although writing that letter was a big decision for him, he was now sure that it was the right decision.

For many months since he had made the shocking discovery of foul play, he had grappled with painful and punishing anxiety over whether or not to reach out to Jane or just let the matter lie. After all, there was no way he could reverse the tragedy of all those years ago and what value was there in upsetting Jane. But finally, blood cried out from the grave for justice. This was something he needed to do. This was right. And he was going to see it through, no matter what. Sipho was no spring chicken. He had not been well for over 18 months, and his doctor's latest diagnosis only served to create a greater sense of urgency and clarity − not only should he act, but he should act quickly.

Sipho held his "Jane Johnson" sign high in the air and focused intensely on the exit sliding doors. His old heart skipped a beat every time they began to open, and he thrust his sign higher, only to drop it down again as he was ignored by the new arrivals. He wasn't sure what he should be looking for, as the last time he saw Jane, she was a young teenager.

He knew how slow customs processing was in his country, but he still arrived early. Now, after over an hour of watching that door, finally, his sign caught the attention of the slim and well-groomed Jane, even after a 16-hour flight. Jane looked at him, their eyes met, and they both knew. Sipho's broad ear-to-ear grin sealed the recognition. Sipho pushed through the crowd, making his way towards Jane as she struggled to haul her luggage across the uneven pavement, navigating a path through the locals who seemed to own the right of way. Or perhaps Jane had suddenly turned invisible on arrival? Somewhere in the distance, Tommy was catching up with the rest of the baggage.

Finally, Jane and Sipho stood face to face. Jane found herself in the grip of a genuinely warm African welcome embrace. Releasing Jane for a moment, Sipho continued to hold her with both arms on her shoulders. He looked deeply into her face with the widest of grins and exclaimed: "Jane, I cannot believe how much like your mother you have grown to be! I am so happy you are here."

Jane looked back into the dark face of her father's friend from so many years ago. Thousands of memories flooded back through her senses in an instant. Sipho's loyalty and faithfulness to her family and her father's ministry were foremost. This was the man, she remembered as a seven-year-old, who no matter how early her family arrived at church on a Sunday morning, was already there with that same smiling face to welcome them. The church set-up had already been completed by him, with everything in place for proceedings to begin — such faithful diligence.

"Sipho, it is incredible to see you again. I wish it were under better circumstances," she said.

"Don't worry, we will get to those details later," said Sipho.

Looking over Jane's shoulder, he saw Tommy approaching, struggling with a carry-on, a large suitcase and two backpacks, already profusely sweating in the African sub-tropical heat of the day. "Do I know this man?" inquired Sipho.

"Yes, you remember, Tommy Cacao?" prompted Jane.

"Of course! Tommy, how could I forget?" said Sipho, throwing his arms around Tommy for another African welcome, oblivious to his arms, still occupied with luggage. "A double blessing to have you both here," said Sipho, unable to hold back his joy.

"Good to see you, Sipho. You haven't aged a day!" complimented Tommy.

"You are too kind, Tommy," replied Sipho. "Come, you must be tired. Let me get to your hotel. Allow me to take one of those bags for you."

Tommy began to untangle himself from his burdens and was about to hand one over when he realised that Sipho was talking to Jane and relieved her from her one obligation instead of him, leaving him to struggle along.

Sipho led the way through the crowded terminal, seemingly getting more respect from the locals than Jane had manage to achieve, across the busy roads to the car park. Jane followed, with Tommy constantly reloading his baggage commitments and trying to keep up.

"Don't worry Jane, I've got it," said Tommy with attempted conviction shrouded in humour.

Jane didn't even break stride or conversation with Sipho as she looked over her shoulder. "Thanks Tommy," she chuckled.

Finally, they reached Sipho's white 1998 Toyota single cab utility bakkie. Jane wondered to herself whether it was the same one he had had when she was last here. Sipho secured the baggage in the truck, and the three of them squeezed into the front bench seat, with Jane in the middle. Sipho was still grinning with overflowing infectious joy as he pulled into the traffic. Jane provided the hotel details. Conversation flowed smoothly as the three of them reminisced about growing up in Africa and the ministry years of the late 1990s and early 2000s.

Jane and Tommy took in the streets of Maputo wide-eyed. Women with babies wrapped in blankets and tied on their backs went about their business briskly and with a strength that overcame the daily toil. Pedestrians, cyclists and cars all contended for the same space in the crowded streets. It seemed like not much had changed at all, almost like they had stepped back in time. Everything still looked so 1970's. Economic progress seemed to be stagnant, or at best, very slow.

"Those were very turbulent years for our country with all the changes in South Africa impacting us as well," said Sipho. "Your father was the right man in the right place at the right time. He seemed to know how to respond to the lift in peoples hopes and aspirations with wisdom and genuine concern, which helped us so much to navigate life and build our families and our futures," he reflected solemnly.

Jane welcomed the change in conversation and took the opportunity to reflect on the reason for their visit. "I just can't tell you how good it is to be here," said Jane. "I was not sure how this would feel. For many years I had made up my mind never to come back. I wish it were under better circumstances, but I feel very strongly that this chapter of our lives was never closed properly, and this needed to happen and was always going to happen."

"Well, I felt the same way," said Sipho. "That's why, after reflecting on everything for a long time, I decided to find you and write. I have someone I want you to meet tomorrow who will make everything clear. You can talk to him yourself, but I must ask you one thing…"

"Of course, anything," committed Jane.

"You must promise me that you will come to this meeting with the same spirit of grace and understanding that was in your father's heart," said Sipho.

"Well, I'm not exactly sure what that means," said Jane "but yes, I will do my best."

"You will know when the time comes, and yes, your best is all that will be required, I am sure," said Sipho. "Well, here is your hotel. I am sure you are both very, very tired. I am going to leave you to rest up, and I will see you at 11 am tomorrow. If you need anything, please just call me. Here is my cell number," said Sipho and handed over a church business card.

"*New Life Community Church,*" said Jane as she read the card. "You've kept the same name all these years!"

"Yes, you will be surprised. We have not felt the need to change much at all — just keep on doing what your father taught us to do," said Sipho, as he pulled into a parking spot.

Tommy began to unload the bags, muttering to himself that he 'knew why he was here.' Jane seemed to be tuned in to his struggle and had quietly been enjoying it, but could not endure seeing him descend into self-pity and picked up the heaviest bag without breaking her chat with Sipho.

"Thank you so much, Sipho. OK, we will see you about 11 then," she confirmed.

"Yes," said Sipho "bye now."

Jane quickly turned to Tommy. "Are you OK with that one then?" she antagonised, pointing to the smallest bag.

"It will be my absolute pleasure," replied Tommy, the meaning not being lost on him at all.

A few steps and the hotel concierge relieved them of their struggles anyway. Tommy and Jane made their way into the hotel foyer and embraced the air-conditioned, colonial-style reception with a not insignificant sigh of relief. Jane was glad she did not skimp on the hotel selection. The Polana Serena Hotel was just what was needed after the long flight. She remembered how her father would take the family there for a night out and allow her mother to enjoy a moment of luxury and a break from township lifestyle.

"I see ministry salaries and benefits have also stayed about the same as this city's 1970s town planning," said Tommy, referring to the absence of air-con in Sipho's truck during the 45-minute journey from the airport.

"Well, I, for one, am looking forward to a cool bath and a deep sleep," said Jane as she signed the hotel registration and collected her key. "Its two pm now, why don't we meet down here about six for a drink and make some dinner plans?" proposed Jane.

"That works for me," said Tommy, collecting his key.

They made their way to the elevator and propped themselves up on opposite sides of the lift, awkwardly stealing gazes at each other in the confined space.

"Thank you for coming, Tommy," said Jane with the gentlest hint of affection. "And not just for carrying my bags. I could not have done this without you."

"It's OK, I wanted to be here," replied Tommy.

The elevator pinged on the eighth floor. "This is me," said Jane. Surprising Tommy, Jane then crossed the floor, kissed him on the cheek and exited the lift.

Tommy looked after her as the doors closed and thought to himself, "Wow, I was not expecting that!" The 12th floor pinged, and he stumbled into the corridor. Finding his way into his room, Tommy collapsed on his bed and pondered the randomness of life, staring into the ceiling fan turning slowly and silently above him. His thoughts bottled Jane's elevator kiss, and he pressed the rewind button more than once.

CHAPTER 10

RECOVERY

Jane ran a bath while she waited for her bags to arrive. 'Travelling would have to be one of the unhealthiest activities you could do,' thought Jane. Over-processed and microwaved meals, confined spaces, stale air, interrupted sleep, shared lavatories – all left her with that yucky feeling. She gave thanks for the simple pleasure of sliding into her bath and pondered what was going on.

Tommy had undoubtedly grown up, she reflected. There was a distinct attractive firmness in the opinions and ideas he had shared over recent days. She felt a particular shift since they caught up for that coffee and lunch a week ago. No longer was he a sounding board for her to bounce off ideas. Now she felt a distinct dependency upon him and an appreciation for his care, concern and commitment to recent events. Normally, her self-resilience and almost trophy-like fierce independence would denounce such leanings. But not this time. The value of this relationship seemed to be rising quickly. She took the next step and quietly admitted to herself that Tommy was attractive, although she was not ready to give in totally to her PA Suzy's observations. Anyway, she counted herself extremely fortunate that he was available and willing to share the emotional challenges of this expedition.

Jane got out of the bath, towelled herself off and turned her thoughts to Sipho as she slid beneath what felt like the softest cool Egyptian cotton sheets. What did he mean by '*Come to this meeting with the same spirit of grace and understanding that was in your father's heart*'? Who was going to be at this meeting that needed '*grace and understanding*? Her father was the most gracious person she ever knew. It would be unfair and difficult to meet his standard. She struggled to remember if she had ever seen her father angry or impatient with anyone. He had the patience of Job, no matter if he was dealing with difficult government authorities, misguided religious people, or even she and her brother Paul. He always had an encouraging word, a softly spoken request or directive. Never demanding, continuously extending grace, a complete gentleman. Especially when dealing with her mother. He never took for granted her commitment to follow him to Africa and support the work, with all of the sacrifices and demands of a foreign country, stripped of the many creature comforts of suburban Sydney. The fatigue of the journey and change in time zones overtook Jane's active mind, and she drifted into a slumber that was deep.

It was after eight pm when Jane awoke with the night breeze drifting through the balcony doors. What was meant to be a nap turned into a prolonged and much-needed sleep. She sat up quickly once she realised the time and reached for her phone. Tommy's text messages of six-thirty pm were polite and fully anticipated the situation, "I guess you needed more rest than you thought. No problem, text me when you are up and about. I'm just catching up on some emails."

"Sorry about that," texted Jane. "Meet you downstairs at 8.30?"

"You know what? You get back to sleep, and I will see you for breakfast at 7am," returned Tommy. "It's late now."

Jane was quietly thankful that Tommy made it easy to renege. It wasn't long before she again embraced the luxury of a deep sleep that conquered the jet lag once and for all.

It was just before five am when Jane stirred back to life. She took her time to get ready, finally unpacking and laying out the different outfit options for the hot tropical climate. She headed downstairs, determined to beat Tommy. But alas, again he was one step ahead of her. There he was, perched up in a window corner of the breakfast café, already with a coffee in hand and buried in a newspaper, drenched in the brightest morning tropical sunshine pouring through the corner window.

"So, you can still read a Portuguese newspaper?" Jane interrupted.

"Well, good morning, sunshine!" greeted Tommy. "Yes, of course, I can still read. Why not?"

"What's on the menu?" said Jane as she took up a seat.

"It's coffee and Portuguese custard tarts for me," recommended Tommy. "I have not had any this good in many, many years."

"OK, I'm in," said Jane. "Did you sleep as good as I did?"

"Nope, I don't think I did, considering how radiant you are looking this morning."

He went on. "A few things kept going around in my head, namely if church leadership was working to dispose of your father, then I wonder if that does go all the way up to Hedgestone? After all, he was actively in charge of all African ministries at the time. You know, I heard he is still in charge and ruling with an iron fist. Never did like the man," said Tommy.

"And then for some strange reason, I could not get your brother Paul out of my head. Tell me, what is he up to these days?"

"I've been a bad big sister," confessed Jane. "I have not spoken to Paul in months. He has been in New York for quite a while now. He is still pursuing his music career in cello, trying out for various orchestras and string quartets. If it's not cello, it's his painting," said Jane. "He is quite good at both. I wish he would concentrate on something and generate a stable income, settle down a bit."

Jane continued, pausing only for another bite of tart or swig of coffee. "These are good. You should order yourself some more," said Jane as she snatched the last one from Tommy's plate. "Paul is a lot like you actually" continued Jane. "He has this deep brooding spirituality thing going on, even a genuine adoration for the life and the person of Jesus — just don't mention the church or church structure to him. I remember watching him play a solo cello piece once. I tell you every note, every bow stroke, he took that cadence deep within himself before releasing the sound with incredible sensitivity, vibrato and respect. He just weighed every moment and took the audience on this amazing journey with him. I really need to catch up with him when we get back. Thanks for the reminder."

Jane's phone buzzed right on cue with a text message from Sipho.

"Sipho's early and out front. Shall we go?" said Jane.

"That's what we came here for. Let's do it," agreed Tommy.

CHAPTER 11

FORGIVENESS CONFRONTED

Sipho was waiting at hotel reception and greeted the approaching Jane and Tommy with wide open arms and a smile almost as wide.

"Good morning!" he welcomed.

"Morning," returned Tommy.

"I trust you are both well-refreshed?" enquired Sipho, as he led the way to his utility vehicle. They bundled in, again with Jane in the middle. "OK, we will go to our church office and talk there."

The frequency of potholes increased the further they drove from the hotel and out of central Maputo. Jane bounced from Sipho's shoulder to Tommy's with a rhythm to which she eventually surrendered. Memories returned as they watched the locals go about their day. Overcrowded mini taxi vans clogged the roads and made their own rules, stopping whenever they wanted, without notice or indicators. Sipho patiently coped with it all without a word. Bicycles contributed to the chaos as they weaved in and out of traffic with an indignant lack of concern for their safety.

"I love it!" said Tommy. "Not that much different to Sydney traffic really. Maybe a fraction more civilised. Sipho, what is your role now with the church?" asked Tommy.

"Well, you see we had a string of American pastors sent over for many years by Arthur Hedgestone, but none of them could localise and adapt like Dale and Dominique — Jane's parents — did. They would only last a few years and complain about the heat, the poverty — all the things they did not have back in America, which I always found strange, considering the container of junk they brought with them. Then they would leave. Eventually, after eight years, the GOF handed the church back to the locals, and now yours truly has taken the work over," said Sipho.

"OK, so you're running the show out here? That's great! You're the right man for the job," complimented Tommy. "Tell me then, are you still affiliated with Hedgestone's global fellowship of churches?" Tommy fished.

"No, not at all. Not since they bought in 'tithing rules' where member churches should give 10% of their income back to the US home church. We felt we could better use that money in local ministries and community support here. And so, eventually they asked us to leave and go our own way, which we were happy to do," continued Sipho.

"Strange," said Jane. "That's just not the spirit of who I remembered us to be."

"Yes, things began to change a lot in the years following your father's death. Everything became tighter — more rules, regulations, reporting and this thing called 'honour tithing' back to Hedgestone," said Sipho. "Once there was a cause, and that cause was people. Your parents were the most exceptional example of that. But then Hedgestone became the cause himself. He was to be ever increasingly revered at conferences, and pastors that did not demonstrate any 'allegiance' in their messages were mysteriously moved on, so many good men were lost to our fellowship," said Sipho with a degree of sadness in his voice, and a slow shaking of his head. "Rather than lose their ministry livelihood and life's work, those that remained became a brotherhood of pathetic sycophants. No surprise they lost their edge and authentic leadership. They became hollow and ineffective. There was no new growth. Their congregations withered over the years, mummified and bound in legalistic allegiance to Hedgestone," said Sipho, almost talking himself into tears as he retold the history.

It wasn't long before they pulled into the compound of the New Life Community Church. Sipho was now on his home turf and seemed to take on a tone of authority as he introduced Tommy and Jane to some local members that appeared to be church employees in security around the church gate. Then on into the office area with more introductions to pastoral care workers, busy on telephones.

Finally, they entered Sipho's 'pastor's cave' office where he ushered them to seats and took up residence behind a humble desk. He reached for his cell phone and made a call and spoke a short, rapid-fire conversation in the local language. "I've asked Nathi Khoza to join us," said Sipho, sounding increasingly solemn.

"This is the man I wanted you to meet," he continued. "Nathi got saved and joined our church about six months ago. He was a deeply troubled man while being very diligent and responsive to anything we asked him to do, always trying to do whatever he could in thankfulness of his salvation and the forgiveness of his sins, which I knew were many as he had spent years in criminal circles. But something seemed wrong. Nathi did not seem to be experiencing any real personal freedom. There seemed to be this huge rock of guilt that so weighed him down," said Sipho with quite a concerned intensity.

Tommy and Jane nodded acknowledgement and found themselves drawn into Nathi's life. Jane had forgotten just how good Africans were at storytelling, so passionate in their facial expressions, and how skilfully they used their eyes to open up your soul, lower your defences and plant their words in your heart. Sipho continued.

"And so, one day I took him out for a coffee, just one-on-one without any brothers around." I told him I didn't need to know all the things that went on in his old life — that was between him and the Lord — but I asked him if he believed he was forgiven. Well, tears began to fill his big dark eyes, and he began to share those things that weighed so deeply on his heart."

Just then there was a polite, light two knocks on the door. "Ah, there is the man himself!" said Sipho, as he lifted his voice and bellowed 'Come in!' towards the door. Nathi opened the door and stood there before making a modest entrance at the beckoning of Sipho. He was about 35 years old, very athletic, tall, softly spoken and simply dressed in jeans and a t-shirt.

"Nathi, meet Tommy and Jane from Sydney in Australia. These are the friends I was telling you about," said Sipho.

Nathi's English was not that good, and it was apparent he had not met that many westerners in his time. "Very pleased to meet you," said Nathi, extending his giant African hand to both Jane and Tommy, with the widest of smiles that seemed to be the local hallmark.

"Please to meet you too," responded Jane and Tommy.

"Take a seat Nathi, join us," said Sipho making every effort to put Nathi at ease. "I was just sharing your testimony with Tommy and Jane. Do you mind if I continue?" said Sipho, politely requesting his acceptance.

"Of course not, please go on," consented Nathi.

"Before he came to the Lord, Nathi, like many young men of his era, got caught up in car hi-jacking gangs. They would go across the border into South Africa and lay in wait along the highways with obstructions across the road at certain hidden places and then assault the drivers and steal their cars, which they would bring back into Maputo for local sale or to the chop shop for parts," said Sipho.

Jane and Tommy continued to listen patiently and earnestly.

"Then, on one occasion, Nathi and his cohorts got a very particular and specific order from their gang leader. They were to wait for a particular green Ford Voyager 4-wheel drive, at a certain place, at a certain time. After a few hours of waiting and ongoing text messages, finally, they saw the approaching target and set their trap. The car braked suddenly on the rise in the highway when confronted with a large truck manifold laid across the road. Nathi and his gang pounced, and in the mayhem, the driver and his companion were shot," finished Sipho.

Jane winced and brought her hands to her mouth. "That's terrible," was all she could say. Glancing at Nathi, she could see he was increasingly disturbed as the story came to its conclusion. The smile was gone, and his head hung low, staring at the floor. Immediately, the compassion in Jane was activated. "Nathi, we've all done things we regret. That's the opportunity of relationship — to be forgiven, to start a new life. Jesus' blood paid the price for all our sins. '*There is now no condemnation for those in Christ Jesus,*'" consoled Jane, proud of herself that she could still remember a scripture or two.

"Jane," said Sipho with a new seriousness, "the people that were hijacked and died that day were your parents."

Jane froze. The blood drained from her face. It was one thing to recite Christian doctrine to a troubled soul. It was another to practice it and forgive her parents' murderer sitting right in front of her. So, this is what Sipho meant when he said she would need all of her father's grace. Conflicting thoughts flashed through her head. She wanted to run out of the room and find a place to sob and pour her heart out. Alternatively, she felt for a second that she should vent and scream about the pain that she had gone through, the disruption to her life, the stolen years of remorse.

Tommy reached out his arm and pulled Jane close. "Jane, I'm sorry," he whispered.

Nathi was now openly weeping with his head in his hands, staring at the floor. "I too am so very, very sorry, Ms Jane. There is no excuse for my actions. I was a young and foolish man with no job and no money. I originally thought I was getting a job with a mechanic. But step by step, I went down this slippery slope of crime and murder. I never, ever got over my shocking actions that day. Those faces haunted me until I meet Sipho, and he shared with me that Paul the apostle was a murderer before he got knocked off his horse," said Nathi.

Sipho let the room bleed for a while longer.

Tears were now streaming freely down Jane's cheeks. There was only one thing she could feel she should do, exactly what her father would have wanted her to do. She slowly lifted her gaze to the miserable Nathi. "Look at me Nathi, she said softly. I forgive you, and Jesus forgives you. Please move on in your new life," said Jane with measured compassion and personal concern for the man.

"Thank you so much," said Nathi after a painful silence. "That means so much to me."

Jane suddenly wanted to know more about that day. "Exactly how did they die?" asked Jane, searching for more details.

"Your father reached for the glovebox after we stopped the car. I thought he was reaching for a gun and I panicked and began to shoot wildly at him. Then the other gang members also opened fire, hitting your mother. Your father then rolled out the car, and I saw there was no gun in his hand but one of your church's gospel tracks. I still remember the scripture text across the top: '*While we were still sinners, Christ died for us*' with a crucifixion image of a bloodied and thorn-crowned Jesus looking out from the flier. I took it out of his hand and have kept it these many years," said Nathi, now an utterly slobbering mess.

Jane nodded silently. "That sounds just like Dad actually," she said, eyes glazed over as if seeing his face before her.

Sipho watched and thought to himself, 'That went particularly well.' Then he caught Tommy looking at him with an 'OK, what now?' raised eyebrow look.

"Jane, we need to continue. Is it OK with you?" asked Sipho.

"There is more?" questioned Jane, wondering what else there could be.

"Only this," began Sipho. "Nathi says when they took back the car to the people that placed the order for the hit, they told them they could keep it. He says they were Americans, and that a friend had seen them here at your dad's church the previous week. I looked up some old records, and I found that we did have some visiting 'brothers' from the US mother church that week. I called them 'Hedgestone's henchmen' – Gary Mitchell and Greg Ruby. We can only join the dots and realise we have got ourselves a story that must be told. Later I will give you your father's letters and emails from around this time. Something is rotten to the core. I believe the time has come to shout from the rooftops what was done in the dark. Jane, I need you to help me do that." Sipho was finished.

Jane, in shock, silently nodded.

Nathi had recovered himself.

Tommy was fired up and breathing deeply, as righteous anger brewed within.

Sipho paved the way forward again. "Coffee anybody?"

CHAPTER 12

A CURIOUS STRANGER

Sipho drove Tommy and Jane to his local café haunt. Nathi excused himsclf and wished Jane all the best, offering to be of any assistance where he could.

The cool of the morning had well and truly passed, and the tropical heat of the day was rising. The trio tossed around various responses to Nathi's story while they waited for their coffees to be served. Tommy and Jane's first and obvious reaction was to go to the police. Sipho explained he had already thought that through. Nathi's story was not enough. And then there were all the complexities around country legal jurisdictions. Going further, if there was some sort of conspiracy that went all the way to Hedgestone, then how could they or anyone prove that? No, the authorities were not an option at this time — not if they wanted to get to the bottom of all of this. They needed to go deeper first.

"Something doesn't make sense in all of this," began Jane. "Why? Why my dad? I mean what sort of motive or reason could there be? You don't just go around knocking off missionaries. What sort of threat could my dad have posed to whoever these people are?"

"Yes, all good questions Jane," said Sipho. "You have to understand the leadership tensions of the day. At the time, Global Outreach Fellowship of Churches had a board of governance that was made up of founding members and long-serving pastors of the original revival growth in the 1970s. That leadership board noticed very clearly that Hedgestone was becoming increasingly isolationist, denouncing nearly every other denomination and frequently teaching that, 'we are the only ones doing anything worthwhile in these last days.'

He broke all ties with mainline fundamental Christian institutions. Everyone else was 'compromised' and had departed from the 'true faith.' They challenged him that preaching this was having a very unhealthy impact upon their congregations — one that they could not support, as it created a culture of self-righteousness, implying that they were 'better' Christians than others. They pointed out to him that some of the institutions he was denouncing had been a part of his Christian heritage — where he first came to salvation and pursued the ministry. They requested that he step aside and take a break after so many years of intense leadership."

"But Hedgestone was unrepentant. He added paranoia to his arrogance, regularly inventing conspiracies against his leadership, both from within his Fellowship of churches and outside — the CIA, the government, especially any Democrat politician. These phantom phobias began to dominate his preaching. Then to paranoia, he added cruel and vindictive persecution against any murmur of disagreement with his ideals. He dissolved the board and with it, any measure of accountability — financial, spiritual or otherwise. He removed those Board of Leadership Pastors from their churches — one by one, like the godfather, he went after them. He sent people into their congregations who caused turmoil and challenge to the local leadership and elders. Pastors were replaced overnight with new pastors that supported Hedgestone — often novices with no experience and little knowledge other than the awareness that with Hedgestone, they would see quick paths to Ministry employment security, turning up in the pulpit the next Sunday without any process or consultation at all. Most churches split. Long-term relationships, and families and friends were torn apart. The purge was on. As far as Arthur Hedgestone was concerned, it was time to sharpen the sword and thrust away with a 'my way or the highway, turn or burn, are you with me or against me' attitude. Normally healthy and refreshing conferences became slanging matches marked by ferociously mocking critiques of departed ministers. Every sermon had a subtext somewhere about the absolute necessity of loyalty to Hedgestone, without which you may never make heaven your home."

"Cruel rules — bad rules with harsh, isolationist and shunning penalties were followed by more rules. The focus forced a culture of rule-keeping. There was no love any more — only laying down of the law. No TV's, no movies, no videos. Break every connection with the outside world. The internet was preparing the way for the anti-Christ, as was all social media. On and on it went… In later years, it calmed down once the purge was complete, including our church here, where we managed to escape with an unchallenged exit, as we were not seen as a financially attractive asset. Plus, your trouble-making dad had already been dealt with. Today the control mechanisms are still there but not as overt or explicit. He had effectively cut back the vine to his 'true believers.'"

Just then, with uncanny timing, Sipho was unexpectedly interrupted. "Hello, Pastor Sipho!" came the voice of a fast-approaching courteous man.

Sipho turned in the direction of the voice and identified one of his long-term church members. Immediately, he went into African pastor-mode. "Hello, my brother, hey, how are you?"

"Well, thank you, Pastor," said the man, inquisitively lingering and wanting to know who the two out-of-towners were.

Awkwardly, Sipho realised he was not going to move on quickly without an introduction. "Oh, please meet two very good friends of ours, Tommy Cacao and Jane Johnson. Jane's father pioneered our church twenty-two years ago. Jane, Tommy — this is Dobbie Doeg," said Sipho.

Dobbie's face went full moon. He stared at Jane with the widest eyes that did not blink. "Your father was Dale Johnson?!" he quizzed in a hushed tone, as if he had met royalty. Jane nodded a humble confirmation. "Wow, I never thought I would have the privilege of meeting you! Dale Johnson is a legend in our township — the brave and courageous Aussie that brought us so many blessings. It is truly an honour," said Dobbie with an overemphasised respect that made Jane feel a little uneasy.

After a longer than comfortable eyeing up of Jane, he turned his attention back to Sipho. "Well, Pastor, I must go. I was just getting a coffee on my way to work. I will see you on Sunday then."

"Yes, OK, Dobbie. And please, don't be late. You are on the roster for set-up duties this week," reminded Sipho.

Tommy watched Dobbie make his way out of the café, but interestingly without a takeaway coffee, he noticed. Instead, he seemed to be urgently making some phone calls. "He sounds like an interesting fellow," commented Tommy.

"Yes, well, he is a little odd. Dobbie has been around a long time but often disappears for months, says he is visiting his family in the homelands" said Sipho.

"Anyway, Sipho, I had heard a few reports and rumblings of different things going on but wow, that certainly fills in lots of the blanks!" said Tommy. "Shocking! It sounds like Hedgestone completely lost the plot."

"But still," said Jane, "how was my dad caught up in all of this?"

"Your dad was a victim of his undeniable integrity. He possessed a moral compass that forever pointed faithfully in the true north direction of Christ's cross. He had an orientation of justice and concern towards his fellow ministry brethren. He asked all the uncomfortable questions to Hedgestone in email after email, and requested meeting after meeting. He had the respect of the vast majority of Fellowship churches across Africa. I've only seen this recently but Hedgestone, at the height of his purge, knew that if he could strategically remove Dale Johnson, then he would save himself from a cascade of dissent from churches in a region that was both remote and distant from his normal influences and tactics. If he didn't deal with Dale, he stood to lose dozens of churches in a breakaway. This, in turn, would damage his missionary fundraising activities — not that the money reached them anyway. And he was not about to allow that to happen. Your fathers' emails and requests for explanations of new rules were fertile ground for Hedgestone's conspiratorial mind to justify his vile plan. He made several demands for Dale's resignation of his church and ministry. Your father refused. If you read the email responses, it's obvious that

Hedgestone was incensed. I believe that was when he hatched his plan. If Dale would not resign, then he would create a circumstance by which he would undermine his ministry. From Nathi's story I don't believe Hedgestone intended to kill your parents, just put them in hospital for a while, out of the way so that he could send in his new man and have a reason to bring him home. But when your father reached for that glovebox and shots were fired, Hedgestone got an outcome that was even better than he hoped for," finished Sipho.

Tommy and Jane sat back in their seats. The pieces were falling into place. Sipho certainly had worked through the jigsaw with remarkable clarity. They both felt overwhelmed by what they had heard. It was going to take some time to work through how they should respond. One thing they knew for sure — Hedgestone needed to be revealed for the fraud he was.

"Let go," said Tommy, finishing his long macchiato with a final swig. "We need to write Hedgestone's tombstone."

CHAPTER 13

THE SWORD OF DOEG

Dobbie Doeg could not believe his good fortune. He had stumbled onto gold, gold, gold… Jane Johnson − here in Maputo! Now that was news − and Doeg knew the value of news like this. Moreover, he already knew who his buyer was for this juicy newsflash.

Doeg had learnt long ago how to trade in information and use the misfortune of others to promote himself in the eyes of wealthy westerners like Hedgestone's henchmen. Snivelling, greasing nepotism was the weaselling way of Doeg. He was addicted to the approval and pleasing of Hedgestone. They had positioned him well to keep an eye on things and report on any movements or developments that might be of interest or a threat to their 'cause'. And reporting that Jane Johnson had turned up was as good a 'development' as he could have ever hoped for.

Something burned with him until he could get it out. He had been briefed on the history of the 'disruptive influence' Jane's father caused many years ago. The sense of urgency was overwhelming in Doeg as he walked briskly through the crowded village streets towards his shack on the edge of town. He closed the door behind him quickly and sat down to scroll through his phone contacts for Greg Ruby. Ruby was known as the Goebbels of GOF and worked his circle of influence brilliantly through the pastoral network to keep an eye who was who and what they were up to. He made men and ministries within the GOF. A quiet word to Hedgestone and a man would be given a leading church with good numbers and healthy cash flow, regardless of character, experience or qualification.

He began to text Ruby, each word like a sharp dagger piercing the bowels of Sipho, Jane and Tommy like they were voodoo dolls in his hands. "Hello, Bro Ruby. It is Dobbie Doeg in Maputo. Can you please call me? You remember the Johnsons and the trouble they caused here in 2004? Well, guess what? Jane Johnson is here with a friend Tommy Cacao meeting with Sipho!"

Doeg clicked send and started counting to ten. He only got to eight before he got a response. He smiled as he received the narcotic approval he craved so deeply.

"Hello, Dobbie, my old friend. So good to hear from you. I will call you within the hour," texted Ruby.

"OK," replied Doeg. He knew it would be a long, long hour. He paced the one room of his concrete-floored shack, cell phone in hand, talking himself through what he would say to Ruby. Then he realised something that terrified him. He had no details on why Jane and crew were meeting. He knew Ruby would want more than just a sighting. What could he say? He had failed to ask Sipho any questions. He kicked himself or not thinking of this. Anyway, nothing he could do now. Just then, his cell phone buzzed in his hand.

"Hello," said Doeg with plenty of friendly expectation in his voice and the best-accented English he could muster.

"Hi Dobbie, this is Greg Ruby, thanks for your text. So hey, you say Jane Johnson is in Maputo meeting with Sipho?" said Ruby, getting straight down to establishing the details.

"Yes, that's right. I bumped into them at a local café," said Doeg. "I thought you might like to know, given all that trouble you told me about from all those years ago."

"Well yeah, that's right. Well, maybe she is just paying a visit to reflect on where she grew up? Do you know why she is in town?" asked Ruby.

Doeg hesitated. "Well, uh…not exactly," stumbled Doeg. "All I can tell you is that they seemed to be in an agitated and serious conversation about something."

"And you have no idea why?" pressed Ruby.

Doeg realised he had not made the most of his opportunity. "Not exactly — no. But if I find out, I will be sure to update you," grovelled Doeg.

"Hey, no problem Dobbie. That would be great. I appreciate you making the call. I'm sure Pastor Hedgestone will be glad to hear of your update. I'll be sure to look you up next time I'm in Africa. Take care, Dobbie," said Ruby, as he signed off.

"Thank you again, Pastor Ruby. I will be sure to be in touch," said Doeg.

'Well, that could have gone better,' he thought to himself as he put the phone down.

'Maybe they think I just wasted their time? Perhaps they think I'm a fool?'

'Only one thing to do,' Doeg told himself. 'I need to find out what Jane and that suave Tommy are doing here.'

Doeg refreshed himself with this self-assigned mission. This had only just begun. He needed to work this event and build his channel with Ruby.

CHAPTER 14

CASCADING DISCOVERIES

It was mid-afternoon by the time Sipho got Tommy and Jane back to their hotel. The heat of the day was maxing out both of them. Sipho did not delay in saying his goodbyes as it was Saturday and he still had not fully prepared for his Sunday message. Jane admired his discipline and priorities and was reminded of her father's similar commitment every Saturday.

They had one more day in Maputo before heading back to Sydney.

"Any plans?" inquired Jane as they made their way to the elevator. "I'm thinking a rooftop swim before dinner would be the best way to unwind after the intensity of this morning. Actually, it's one of the reasons I picked this hotel. Care to join me?" asked Jane.

Jane had Tommy's attention. "That is an excellent idea, Jane," said Tommy, not wanting to sound too keen but neither wanting to lose out on the opportunity.

Together, they entered the lift, which they had to themselves, and selected their floors. Jane stood opposite Tommy with her lips pursed together and a bemusing frown on her face, looking directly at Tommy.

"What?" asked Tommy, puzzled by the look on Jane's face.

"Sorry, it's nothing," said Jane. "I just wanted to tell you that I so very much appreciate you making the effort to come with me and be with me through all of this."

Jane's elevator floor pinged. "So, I will see you at the pool in 10 mins?" she checked again.

"Sure," said Tommy. "And Jane, I am happy I came as well, so don't think too much about it. See you soon," he squeezed in as the elevator doors closed behind Jane.

'OK,' thought Tommy to himself, as he made his way to his room, 'what do I do with that? Do I take it that Jane appreciates me being here or that Jane appreciates me being me?'

'Don't try and answer that question now,' he told himself. 'Just enjoy the moment.' After all, Jane was right — it had been an intense morning.

He quickly changed into some board shorts and a singlet, grabbed his room card, sunnies and a book he had been determined to make progress with this trip, and headed back to the elevator.

The doors opened, and he was taken by surprise by Jane equally decked out for a sunny session. "Dang! I thought I would beat you to it!" she said playfully.

"Sorry," played along Tommy. "You're a fraction too slow."

"I was waiting for ages for the lift," said Jane. "I was hoping to get there before you and bag a nice spot for us and a cold drink for you."

"Well, thank you for thinking of me," returned Tommy. "I'm sure we can find one together."

The doors opened to the rooftop pool, and they were both pleasantly surprised that it was not as crowded by guests as they might have expected. There were plenty of options to set up camp in one of the cabanas around the pool. Tommy let Jane lead the way and choose a spot.

"This one has options for both shade and sun," she said as she claimed her sun lounger with her towel and bag. "You take the sunny deck since you've got the Mediterranean olive complexion, and I'll protect my fair skin in the shade."

"Yep, good poolside real estate," agreed Tommy as he pulled off his shirt and thongs and took up residence on his side. Jane stripped down to her modest but very shapely swimsuit. Tommy could not help but admire how Jane had undoubtedly looked after herself over the years, but in no way did he want her to know what he was thinking, so he disciplined his eyes with an 'above the shoulders' line of vision policy.

"Now how about that drink you promised? A cold Asahi would be just fine," he prompted.

"Coming right up," said Jane, making her way to the bar.

Tommy settled in to soak up the sun. This was a nice break from winter in Sydney, he thought to himself.

Jane returned, sat down on her lounger in front of Tommy and placed the drinks on the table between them. "Here you go, Mr Tommy, please consider my debt paid."

"Well, thank you," said Tommy, reaching immediately for the cold glass.

"Now, I have one more favour to ask," said Jane with irresistible puppy dog eyes.

"Oh, now I get it," said Tommy, nearly spilling his drink. "And I thought this was because you truly liked me," he challenged playfully.

"Well, of course, I do. You know that by now, right? I know you do. Don't worry. This doesn't require carrying any heavy baggage. I would like you to come with me to visit my parents' grave before we leave tomorrow. I realised that I've never visited it since they died. I feel terrible, and a little overwhelmed. I'm not sure how I will handle it, but I know I need to do it and whatever happens, I will handle it better if you are there," she confided with a sincerity that caught Tommy entirely off-guard.

He suddenly felt a little guilty. "Of course, I will. That's not a favour," Tommy corrected, "I would like to be there for you."

For a fleeting moment, their eyes meet, and both Tommy and Jane caught a glimpse into each other's hearts.

Jane was the first to shut it down with a polite but dismissive, "Thank you. Anyway, what are we going to do with this Hedgestone when we get back?"

Tommy was relieved at the change in conversation direction. "Only one thing to do. Expose him. The western church is out of control — no boundaries, no governance — a law unto themselves. Self-preservation rules the day. What we heard today was the fullest extension of that self-serving spirit running in its own direction. How did the church become so commercialised and corporatised that it could conceive such a strategy?" Tommy argued.

"This is why I am happy to stand back from it all and quietly attend a local small connect group where we get back to basics like sharing and caring, doing life together — not in a shallow way, but with the longevity of relationship in mind. Do you know I read the other day that evangelical Christians stay an average of 22 months in one congregation before looking for someone else to stroke their ego? We have this transient church population that creates a shallowness and almost 'artificial holiness,' if I can call it that.'

"Well, you certainly worked that out before I did," said Jane with a degree of surrender. "I suppose I would call myself only a casual attendee at the Sydney church. I just felt loyal in some way to Dad. I've never been greatly involved in any ministry or activity. I just kept busy with my work. Now I feel sick that I am connected in any way with Hedgestone's network of churches. I suppose I need to get out of there now."

"No!" said Tommy. "If we are to get to Hedgestone, then I think we are going to need you to stay on the inside for a while longer."

"OK, yes, working from the inside out might be helpful. But this is so messed up. Whatever happened to a church where ministry is authentic, and congregations are community? When did we start to become kingdom proprietors rather than humble pilgrims? Why are insecure men trying to 'own God' rather than 'serve people'? How come we have forgotten that we are on a journey to that heavenly Zion and stop trying to set up a perfect life in a temporal world? When will we be reminded of the privilege we have to use the gold but not touch the glory? How did the western church get into this mess? Can someone please tell me how Jesus would do Church in this day and age?" questioned Jane.

Jane was now speaking beyond her sphere of knowledge, almost prophesying like some seer looking into the unknown. She was putting into words a consolidation of thought glimpses that had built up over many years that seemed to be activated by Tommy's reflections. Together, they were like two excited scientists in a laboratory, uncovering and documenting observations that no one else they knew of dared to vocalise or speak out loud. This was not stuff you would find in the church newsletter.

Tommy's mind was building upon the thoughts Jane had just laid out. "You know what I think, Jane?" he prompted. "This is not just about vindication for your parents — it's bigger than that. We have the opportunity to make a statement that shakes up once and for all how these corporatised mega-churches function and deal with people, and I get that for every bad egg there are 100 sincere ministries."

"Sounds like we've got a job to do when we get back to Sydney. But first things first. That pool has been calling me for a swim. Coming in?" she said to Tommy and made her way to the edge for a dive into the deep end. Tommy was not far behind.

CHAPTER 15

GRAVEYARD MOTIVATIONS

Once the sun went down, Tommy and Jane finished up at the pool and found their way to a local Portuguese BBQ peri-peri chicken street vendor not far from the hotel. There was something almost intoxicating in the warmth of the tropical evening, and the hustle and bustle of locals finding their way home with an end of day slowness. They both stole themselves away from the seriousness of the current cause for a moment and blended into the local scene almost seamlessly. They ate quietly without much discussion and watched the colourful people parade from their street bench stools, sensing that to speak would interrupt the indulgence of the moment.

The next day, both Tommy and Jane rose early to pack for the return trip home. Their flight was scheduled for late afternoon. Jane had arranged for their taxi to first take them past the cemetery on the outskirts of town.

Tommy's ability to converse with the taxi driver in fluent Portuguese proved to be very handy as the driver seemed insistent on taking the scenic route and run the meter longer than was necessary. They arrived at the cemetery, and again Tommy was able to engage with the admin office to find their way to Jane's parents' plot. After 15 mins of walking and navigating through the small and winding random pathways, they finally stood before a very simple and humble gravestone.

Jane reached for Tommy's hand as she read the inscription. She was particularly drawn to the scripture texts used in the narration.

Firstly, *2 Cor 5:8 To be absent from the body is to be present with the Lord* and then underneath that, *Thess 2:2 For you yourselves know, brethren, that our coming to you was not in vain.*

She wondered who chose those texts. Maybe it was Sipho? But if she was to sum up her parents' lives, she could not think of anything more appropriate. The legacy of her parents' ministry was certainly not in vain, and nobody was able to rob them of their eternal reward, even if they were cut down in their prime years of effectiveness.

"Tommy, did you read those texts?" Jane asked.

"Yep. It says it all, doesn't it?"

"Certainly does." Jane took a snapshot of the stone. She found a place to sit on a rock under a tree. Her eyes glazed over as she stared at her parents' resting place. All of the 'whys' started flooding back. Tommy stood at a distance, not wanting to intrude. They both absorbed the quietness, interrupted only momentarily by the birds that sang quietly in the trees above and the leaves that rustled in the wind.

Finally, Jane stood up. "We need to leave," she said with a clear decisiveness.

It was evident to Tommy that lingering by a grave pondering all of the 'why's' and interrogating all of the 'could-have-been' scenarios was a temptation Jane was not willing to indulge in. Did the visit give rise to a closure transaction? 'Not really,' thought Tommy. He knew Jane too well now — closure would only be possible once those responsible were held accountable for what was buried in that place. Not just the two people, but a whole family's life story and work of passion. It was not with closure, but determination that Jane walked away with in her heart.

The taxi trip to the airport was far less eventful than that to the cemetery. Both Jane and Tommy went into travel zombie mode again as they worked through the check-in, security and customs formalities. It wasn't long before they were finding their seats for the connecting flight back to Johannesburg. It was seven pm by the time they were on-boarded for Sydney.

Feeling refreshed after a snooze on the first flight, Tommy felt up for a chat. "OK, so what is the plan from here? Any ideas? Do we go back to our day jobs as if nothing happened?" he prompted Jane.

"Well, I think that that's exactly what we do. No big moves, no announcements, no confrontations. We pretend nothing happened until we dig in deeper and find out who is who in the zoo in Arthur Hedgestone's world. We don't have anything that links Hedgestone completely to any of this."

"What do we do when we are in those situations commercially? We wait. We prompt, we prod, we research, we dig. And I reckon, we pray. We are going to need some divine intervention and direction to work through this. It can't be something we orchestrate. Maybe this has to be something God wants us to do. More than me justifying my parents, the Lord has to deal with his Church. They are his leaders. It's his job to discipline and bring change. He is more capable than us in cleaning out his church of hirelings and vipers, just as Jesus overturned the tables of the merchants in front of the temple. Something tells me it won't be long before they come to us. I got a very uncomfortable feeling from that Dobbie. Let them come. Play dumb. We are just old friends that went back to our childhood home for a holiday."

Tommy got a glimpse as to why Jane earned the big bucks in her practice: Insightful planning. A wisdom beyond her years, enabling her to traverse the nuances of knowing before the facts become clear. She was able to navigate the shadowy lands of deceit and deception, emerging in the clear at the right time and the right place.

"I can work with that. Tell me what you want to do, but I think I can begin the research end for you. Finances, structure, GOF governance. What makes Hedgestone strong? What are his weaknesses? Let me see what's in the public domain and what isn't."

"OK," Jane agreed. "Anyway, what is on the menu for dinner?"

Why people still looked forward to mealtime on aeroplanes, Tommy could not understand. The portion size was getting smaller and smaller, and the quality was moving in the same diminishing direction, despite the fancy titles and ambitious descriptions on the menu handouts. At any rate, they made their choices, settled into a few movies before sleep overtook them both, as their Qantas flight powered eastward.

However, 10,000 kilometres away, Greg Ruby had no intention of sleeping. He had been trying to get hold of Hedgestone since his last chat with Dobbie Doeg. Despite leaving several messages, he had not yet received a call back. Now, after Sunday service finished, when he knew Hedgestone would be unwinding, he picked his moment. He was right. The phone only rang three times before it was picked up.

"Hello," boomed Hedgestone, with a heavily accented 'don't-waste-my-time' emphasis.

"Pastor Hedgestone? Hi, its Greg Ruby here. I hope I'm not interrupting?"

"Greg, great to hear from you. Not at all. How was your Sunday?"

"Well, you know, one of those SOS services. Same old songs, same old sermons, same old sheep…"

"I've had plenty of those, Greg. Sometimes success is to just keep turning up. Anyway, how can I help?"

"Look, I had a call from Africa on Friday. You might remember the works we had in Maputo, started many years ago by the Johnsons? Also, some of the troubles we ran into when they began cultivating what we might call 'alternative views' of leadership, finances and your good self…"

Hedgestone needed no prompting to remember. He knew exactly what had gone down in Maputo 12 years ago. "Oh yes, the Johnsons. An unfortunate event…"

"Well," continued Ruby, "I left in place a contact there many years ago, a man named Dobbie Doeg, to keep me in the loop if things ever got 'disruptive' with Sipho Mbane, who took over the church and took it out of the Fellowship, if you remember? He still has influence over other nationals we have in our fellowship there. Anyway, Dobbie tells me a curious thing. Apparently, the Johnson's daughter, Jane, from the Sydney church, was in Maputo with Tommy Cacao, who also grew up in the church there in Maputo. He says they seemed to be having all-day meetings with Mbane. I've also done some research on Mbane, and he seems to be asking a lot of people a lot of questions about the incidents surrounding the carjacking of the Johnsons."

"I see," mused Hedgestone. "Well, the passing of the Johnsons was a tragedy for us all. I'm sure there is nothing of concern here, but please stay in contact with your Dobbie, and if he feels concerned about anything, please let me know how I can help. Do we understand each other?"

Ruby knew Hedgestone was forever being the politician and protecting his position. Although he knew he trusted him, he was not about to say anything that would ever compromise his position. "Sure, we understand each other. OK well, you enjoy the rest of your evening and please pass on my regards to Beatrice."

"Thank you, Greg. Bye now," said Hedgestone, cautious of not allowing such an exchange to continue any longer than necessary. Hedgestone picked up the pencil he kept near the house phone and wrote on his notebook beside it, "Johnson" with a thick underline. This was going to be his first task of the new week ahead.

CHAPTER 16

CURIOUS VOICEMAIL

It was late on Monday afternoon local time when Tommy and Jane's flight touched down in Sydney. While they did manage to get some sleep, they were both feeling the fatigue of the gruelling 12-hour flight. However, this was quickly offset by the joy of being home after a short but emotionally and physically draining African adventure. Once they got through baggage and customs, Tommy found himself being personally challenged in trying to remember where he parked his car.

"The carpark was empty when we left," said Tommy, trying to excuse his blunder.

"Don't worry, I took a picture while you were getting the bags out of the car," said Jane, sliding through her phone photos.

"J3-10!" she announced victoriously. "That way!" she directed, pointing back the way they had come. "Of course, some say that women are spatially and geographically challenged. Perhaps that was a rumour started by a university professor who could never find his car on the college campus."

"OK, OK, thank you. You're smart. I'm dumb. I surrender! I just want my bed," yawned Tommy with a convenient, if not exaggerated, tiredness.

Jane accepted the tacit acceptance of her usefulness and wisely knew when no more words were necessary. "There's your beast," she said, heading towards his white Peugeot. "I know, I know — your eyes are also very, very tired. Poor fellow," she taunted.

This time, Tommy knew words would not advance his position at all. He fumbled in his carry bag for his keys. 'No, no, don't tell me I've misplaced my keys as well,' he thought to himself. His fingers dug deeper and emerged with the car keys before Jane could circle for another barb. 'Thank God!'

He popped the boot and loaded the bags, and they were on their way to the exit gate – with a paid ticket! 'At least I got that right,' he thought to himself.

The journey home was mostly uneventful and without conversation. That was until Jane switched her phone off aeroplane mode and a flood of pings sounded off as local messages came in and she worked through her voicemail.

"Hmm, that's strange," she noted. "Listen to this:"

Hello Jane, its Claire Endor from Pastoral Care at Hope Valley Church. I heard you were recently in Africa? How exciting! I'd love to hear all about it. Let me know when we can catch up for a coffee.

Jane instinctively did not like Claire. Although they did not have much contact, she often felt like she was being manipulated when around Claire. And her husband – what a mouse! Always following orders and guarding every word he spoke so as not to be taken as threatening of her 'spiritual leadership' in the church.

"What's that? What's so strange?" inquired Tommy.

"I've got a voicemail from Claire Endor from church who I haven't spoken to in over a year."

"And who is Claire Endor?" Tommy quizzed further.

"Well, she is in charge of Pastoral Care. Says she wants to catch up for a coffee and 'see how I'm doing.' She's using a 'we are best buddies' sort of tone. I wonder how she knew where I was? Maybe she rang Suzy at my office?"

"I told you they would come to us! But I never expected it to be so quick! And not Claire. Wow! Do you reckon Hedgestone is already on the move? How? Or merely a coincidence, and we are just tired and paranoid?"

"OK, well, I'm impressed…" said Tommy.

"You know what? I reckon it was that Dobbie Doeg. I had a strange and uncomfortable feeling when we bumped into him at that café with Sipho. He didn't seem genuine. Anyway, only one way to find out. I hope you can remember some moves from your drama and acting lessons because you are going to have to be in full-on 'hollywoodin' mode. Be interested in her — 'Thank you for your concern. Yes I would love to catch up,' etc. etc. Draw her into your confidence. Don't hide or be defensive. What do you think?"

"I think we have to stop living in each other's head. This is scary. That's exactly what I was thinking. Don't worry — I'm up to it. From what I remember of crafty Claire, she is also going to have a carefully constructed plan and dialogue. Game on! Let's play!"

Tommy pulled in front of Jane's apartment block and got out to unload her bags.

"Well, right now, you should forget about all that and get yourself some rest. There is no hurry to respond."

"Good advice, Mr Cacao. You too. And we will talk tomorrow sometime?"

"Sure," said Tommy as Jane surprised him with a warm, close embrace and a kiss on the cheek.

"Again, I want to thank you for coming with me. I have no idea how I would have handled all that on my own," said Jane, looking deep into Tommy's eyes.

Tommy did not reply. Just gazed back into Jane's baby blues.

"OK, until then?" said Jane and headed for the entrance to her apartment block.

"Sure," said Tommy gazing after her. He closed the boot, got back into his car and pulled out into the peak hour wintery Sydney traffic. He peered ahead and could make out the blurred outline of the bridge against a backdrop of dark clouds. He pondered whether to take the harbour tunnel or the bridge. He decided on the foggy bridge. He could do with the visual imagery of the magnificent harbour that was inspiring in any weather. He slowly passed the sandstone tower end and absorbed the symmetry of the steel girders passing around and overhead.

To his right, he could make out the shell shapes of the Opera House. This is what he needed, he thought to himself. A birds-eye view of the landscape in which he found himself, a way to locate himself in the circumstances. On an emotional level, he discovered that Jane had found her way into his heart like no one else ever had. Further, that this affection was growing and slowly taking possession of his waking thoughts. Then on an integrity level, he felt the burden and intensity of a righteous cause. He felt offended that the goodness and trust of ordinary and humble Christians like Jane's parents, was being taken for granted and abused by a self-serving leadership that ruled via threats and intimidation and had created something that was an eternity removed from the intention of what he knew as a pattern New Testament church.

He continued the crossing and drew close to the end of the sandstone tower. Just as the bridge rose over the waters, so too did he feel a desperate need for an elevated perspective, to be able to see things from far above what he could currently see in the fogginess of the ground zero landscape. If he were able to clearly navigate the scene before him, Tommy knew he would need to reach back to the God he had experienced as a teenager, growing up in the tumultuous third world economy of Mozambique, a country ravaged by civil war. A time when things could have gone either way for him. He could have shut out God's love and promise and continue to go his own way on a downward spiral, or he could turn and receive and stop the drag of an empty, hopeless void that no lifestyle or drink or drug or person could fill. Glimpses and thought sketches of Isaiah 55:9 began to surface within Tommy. Perhaps it was even from a sermon Jane's father had preached long ago.

For as the heavens are higher than the Earth, so are my ways higher than your ways, and My thoughts higher than your thoughts.

'OK, I get it, Lord,' he said to himself. 'So, give me Your perspective, show me what You can see, direct me in the next steps before me. How do you want these things to proceed?'

Tommy was a mature enough Christian who knew the importance of involving the Lord in life situations as soon as they emerged. He didn't expect flashes of lightning bolt answers or thundering voices from heaven. But he did expect that as he sought the Lord early in a situation and provided the opportunity for Him to get involved, that he could eagerly expect Him to act and make a way when none was immediately evident.

As he pulled into his driveway, he took comfort in his history and relationship confidence with the Lord. He would cease from undue worry and concern and allow God room to move before him.

Tiredness began to overtake him as he dropped his bags inside his townhouse and crashed out on his couch, completely forgetting that he was supposed to resume his pet duties and feed his co-tenant, Neo the cat, his 'Whiskers' and water.

CHAPTER 17

DARKNESS ACTIVATED

Claire Endor had a difficult past, to say the least. A toxic brew of a bitterly broken family at a time when she was entering her formative teenage years had made a deep and dark etching on a young heart — one that was rapidly turning to stone.

She punished herself often with self-inflicted harm and increasingly noted that she didn't feel the pain because it was nowhere near the intensity of the emotional pain she felt from having broken parents who were without natural affection towards her, and a shattered security with nowhere to call home anymore.

When the cutting and scarring no longer held any attraction or distraction for her, Claire immersed herself in reaching out to dark spirits in the hope that perhaps they could break the dismal reality she called life. She had progressively determined within herself that if life was bad to her, then she was fine with finding out where bad lived and owning it for herself. Why be on the receiving end of bad when you can dish it out to others?

Throughout her high school years, she slowly descended down treacherous paths, choosing companions like herself that just wanted to be bad. Bad became a competition, and she had no interest in coming second. The usual suspects of sex, drugs and alcohol were merely training wheels for her. At 16, she found another entry point to go even darker and deeper.

Two high school friends invited her over to what they thought would be their chance to gain favour with Claire, who by now seemed to be well-connected, with an abundance of older male acquaintances. This particular night, they thought they would impress Claire with their ouija board antics out in their country yard, but Claire had not come to play board games. Ten minutes into the session, she caught sight of their pet rabbit in a cage close by. She went over and admired how cute and cuddly he looked.

"Do you mind if I have a hold?" Claire asked.

"Sure, go ahead," said her friends not imagining where this might go.

Claire opened the cage and reached in to pull the bunny out and held it close to her chest, walking back to where their ouija board session was in progress. "He is so soft," said Claire resuming her cross-legged place, sitting on the grass.

"It's your turn, Claire."

"Good," said Claire and held the unsuspecting rabbit over the board and snapped its neck in a single movement with her bare hands. Before the girls could respond, Claire slammed the bunny down on the board, picked up a rock and smashed open its head, splattering its brains across the girls. She then pulled out a knife from her boot, slit its throat and poured the blood over the board and threw the carcass to the owner with its little legs still kicking.

"C'mon, let's get on with it," said Claire. "You do want to play, don't you? Everyone knows you can't bring up a spirit without a blood sacrifice. Or would one of you like to take the place of Roger Rabbit?"

That night, Claire didn't show it to her unsuspecting acquaintances, but she deeply shocked herself as much as she did anyone else. She felt an unbelievable rush that she could execute such a move without remorse. Claire learned what it felt like to take authority over others by being willing to do what others were not even thinking could be done. And she liked it. Manipulating others, dominating their will, getting people to do what she wanted, being feared amongst peers – this was finally where Claire felt she belonged.

Years passed, and Claire grew her skills in the dark crafts. The internet opened up a whole new world of connecting with covens, and circles of power and influence. Be it online or an exclusive city bar, she knew where to find her prey. Her ability to manipulate the will of others, both emotionally and intellectually, grew fast. She had mastered the beguiling serpent spirit of seducing words that moved individuals to alternative untruths with question after question.

She fought intentionally and successfully for the attention of their eyes and focused them in the view that suited her purpose. No school was necessary. It had nothing to teach her about life. She worked through multiple relationships with many business professionals, both guys and girls — she didn't care. 'Just let me find where the money lives,' she told herself. Whatever emotion was necessary – appreciation, significance, damsel-in-distress, sexual prowess, affection – she could supply it in convincing doses. Deceit and manipulation unlocked the treasures of luxury holidays, fashion, an impressive cache of jewellery, and cash living allowances often beyond her expectation.

That was until she met Davis Dudley. Dudley was smart. He saw Claire coming and knew what she wanted. Claire thought that perhaps Davis was different. Not only in the fact that his personal fortune was way more than anything she had touched so far, but that maybe this time, a real relationship might be possible. Perhaps she could leave behind the bad and find something real in life — something good, just for once?

But Dudley had no such intentions. He used Claire's sex goddess presence to accompany him to many business functions and dinner partners with influential officials in his merchant banking enterprise. Dudley knew how to manage risk. He never let Claire see the gold or get anywhere near it. Yes, she was useful in building networks of relationships, and yes, the live-in sex suited him fine, but a few too many questions about things that didn't concern her, and the risk level began breaching his comfort zone.

Late one Thursday evening, she came home to Dudley's bridge and harbour views apartment to find her bags packed for her in the entrance hall. Looking up, she noticed Dudley's executive assistant, Cath McPherson, standing in the lounge with two security guards behind her.

"Good evening, Ms Endor," said Cath with all of the frozen charm she could muster for the moment — a moment she had long waited for. She had not liked Claire from the moment they'd first met.

The feeling was very mutual. The battle for influence with Dudley had long been played out, but Claire had finally met her match.

"Mr Dudley no longer requires your services and wishes to part company in a positive and amicable manner," said Cath with an absolute resolve that effectively conveyed that no objection or discussion would be entered into. "You will find a generous allowance in this envelope that communicates both Mr Dudley's gratitude and generosity. Please, may I have your apartment key?"

If Jane had found a way to ignore pain and anger by always leading to inflict it on others first, this was not going to be an occasion where it would be effective. McPherson's words penetrated deep into the rock that had taken up residence where her heart used to be and smashed all of her defences to pieces.

Jane briefly looked at the well-dressed security attendants and realised she did not know them and could have no influence on the situation. She glared at Cath while she held out her hand to collect the envelope, refusing to take a step towards receiving it from her. Cath was equally not willing to take a step in the unspoken standoff but happily obliged the handover duty by passing the envelope to one of the security attendants to pass to Claire. Claire clinched the envelope and turned for the door, not realising the security gentlemen had not let go of the envelope.

"Apartment key please, Ms Endor," requested Cath with triumphant undertones and the authority of a private school principal. Without looking at her, Claire reached into her jacket pocket, handed over the key and headed for the door.

Claire was angry — crazy mad and emotionally infuriated. "How dare he do this to me!"

But this time, she was utterly powerless. This time she had been taken down before she could get close enough to the riches.

She waited until she was in the back of the cab before opening the envelope.

Now the emotional volcano completely erupted. "Twenty thousand dollars! Is that all?!" Claire shook her head in disbelief.

It took only three weeks for Claire to blow the $20,000 on riotous living and designer drugs. Her ability to wield her charms to catch new opportunities no longer seemed to be effective. Once again, she found herself in a place where life had seemingly cast her down. No pursuit of the dark arts was of interest to her any more. She hated herself and the world.

She began to eat her way through her depression. Within three months, her trim and taut physique was no longer easily recognisable thanks to the addition of nine kilograms to her otherwise small frame. More often than not, she cried herself to sleep. Her only friend seemed to be the regular checkout girl at her local supermarket, always with a bright smile and ready for a conversation on how her week had been, and asking if there was anything else she could do for her.

On one particular occasion, Claire had had enough of the friendliness. "My week has been shit, OK! My whole life has been shit and NO! You and your miserable checkout chick life cannot help me with anything!" Claire then stormed off from the counter without taking her bags. Somewhat shocked and challenged, the brave young teenage girl closed up her register, picked up Claire's groceries and pursued her.

"Excuse me madam, but you left these behind," she said as she caught up.

"You again!" glared Claire. "Don't you get it? Leave me alone. I don't want the groceries. Look at me, can't you see I don't need any more food?!" shouted Claire through clenched teeth.

"OK, OK, I get that you're upset. Calm down. Take your groceries. You paid for them," the unswerving checkout attendant said with yet another smile. She continued, "I know you don't think I can help, but I think I know someone who can."

"Here is my number," she said, before pulling out a card from her pocket. Then having completely disarmed Claire with her directness and uninvited concern, she put both hands on her shoulders, looked into her dark eyes and said with an undeniable boldness: "Jesus wants to set you free from the hatred and anger that has taken a stranglehold on your life."

Before Claire could raise her protest and unleash abuse, the unnamed girl had turned and left. She glared after her with piercing aggression before turning on her heel and making her way back to her apartment with the grocery bags. All the way there, Claire internalised her anger, screaming her outrage at the memory of the girl that dared put the name of Jesus in her face. Finally, she reached home, slammed the door behind her, went into her bedroom and screamed into her pillow: "Jesus!? How dare that rude, insolent bitch say that to me! Where was Jesus when I was trashed and rejected by my parents? And how come he never showed up in my world of pain and hurt for six years?"

That was when her Damascus moment happened. Unannounced and unexpected, but as clear and real as all of her pain, she heard a still and small but powerful voice in her heart say, "Claire, I've been waiting for you since the day you were born. Turn to me now, and I promise you a new heart and a new life. Just ask me for it, and it's yours. Just judge yourself and the decisions you've made. Love can take the place of pain, just as the morning takes the place of the night".

For the first time in many years, Claire stopped and listened. 'Love can take the place of pain? Seriously? Well, that's what I want. That's what I've always wanted.'

What followed was the miracle every human heart needs to have. She cried her heart out for two hours. She incrementally received the possibility that life could be different. She spoke the name, silently at first, but then audibly, and asked for his promise.

The rest of Claire's transformation is an amazing salvation story. She rang Beth, the young woman from the supermarket, made it to church that Sunday, and began the journey. It took some months for her to unload all the junk she had been carrying around for so long, but altar after altar, week after week, Claire grew clean and whole and thrived in a spiritual culture of righteousness and truth.

Simple things began to make so much sense. She eventually met and married a soft and sensitive man, Peter, who cared about her in a way she had never experienced. She delighted in taking on pastoral support roles in her local church and the ability to influence others positively with her testimony. But then, some years later, things shifted in an unhealthy direction when she heard Pastor Arthur Hedgestone preach at a conference and was later introduced to him by a church colleague.

'Wow,' she thought to herself, 'this guy has the same power and influence I used to have. He uses the same tone and tools I used to use.'

That was it. Claire was hooked on Hedgestone. She listened to every podcast, read every article he wrote, went to every one of his US conferences, hungered for the measure of his message and the pattern of his words.

They connected often, and Claire was promoted quickly through church leadership ranks and onto paid staff. As was Hedgestone's way with many others, he made her feel she was a trusted ally in the regionally distant Australia from his US base.

That's why Claire Endor was only too pleased to receive his call and accept his request to find out what it was that Jane Johnson had been up to in Mozambique.

"Find out, do whatever you need to do, and let me know, as soon as you can," barked Hedgestone with a raspy abruptness that made Claire realise this was no ordinary pastoral assignment.

"Whatever you need, Pastor Hedgestone," responded Claire, "I'm onto it now."

CHAPTER 18

HEARTS AND PURPOSES CONNECTED

Jane had intentionally set her alarm an hour early for her return-to-work day after the Africa break. Not so much because she wanted to rise earlier than usual but to help break the nasty time zone difference with some half-sleep snooze time. Despite her plan, when the phone alarm charm 'night owl' went off, it felt brutal. Nonetheless, she eventually broke through the weariness, arose and got ready to face the day.

On arriving at her office, Jane was warmly greeted by her faithful and supportive EA Suzy. "Oh, welcome back, Ms Johnson! Boy, are you the talk of the town at the moment! Off to Africa with the dark and mysterious Tommy Cacao. How did it all go? Anything I need to know?"

"Just visiting family, Suzy. Yes it was a wonderful break and thank you for asking," said Jane.

"Well, I've just emailed you a Word doc with an update of important people and messages from while you were away. Can I get you a coffee, Jane? Most importantly, you have a partner meeting at 3.30 pm this afternoon."

"Yes please that would be entirely wonderful," responded Jane, taking sanctuary in her office and closing the door. Jane quickly dealt with urgent client matters and calls before working through Suzy's messages list. She was expecting to find a call perhaps from Claire Endor to follow on from the message left on her phone, but there was nothing. Jane decided to return the call after lunch, not wanting to appear too keen.

"Claire Endor speaking," said Claire with a saccharin sweetness.

"Oh, hi Claire, its Jane Johnson, you left a message on my phone last week."

"Jane, well, how are you? Yes, I did call. I tried your office to see if you could help on some church business matters regarding a lease we want to renegotiate, but they told me you were on leave in Africa and so I thought it's been so long, we should catch up for a coffee anyway. Is there a time that works for you this week?"

'Hmm, she disguised the purpose of the call quite well,' thought Jane. "How about tomorrow afternoon, at 3 pm, the Black Cat Café just near my office? Could that work?" she said.

"Absolutely, that's fine. "I'll see you then."

"OK, bye now," said Jane, wanting to keep it short and sweet.

Jane got busy that afternoon, trying to concentrate and relocate herself in her work life. This was not so easy. Conversations from the previous week kept contending for her thoughts, as did the faces of Sipho, Nathi and others from that surreal time. Then there was the visit to the cemetery where her parents were buried. It just was not right that they were disposed of in such a cold and callous manner by Hedgestone and the Fellowship.

At 6 pm, Jane began wrapping up at the office. She had held herself back all day, but now she felt she had waited long enough. Something had been increasingly burdening her since she got back and she needed to unload it. She felt that were things she needed to share with Tommy, but then questioned whether it was just the travel drag and a touch of back-to-work syndrome.

She decided to text Tommy anyway. "Hi, how was your day? Can I call you at seven? Just leaving the office now."

Jane was halfway to the train station when she got Tommy's reply, confirming that seven was fine. By the time she got home, she still had 20 minutes before the call. She quickly considered her dinner options, which were not good given that she had not done any shopping since returning, before deciding two-minute noodles and toast was all she had time for. She was looking forward to hearing Tommy's voice. After spending a week in each other's presence every day, she had missed him.

Jane put the phone on speaker and dialled Tommy while she sat down with her noodles at her small kitchen table.

"Jane?" Tommy answered.

"Yes, it's me, so how are you?"

"Yeah OK, all things considered. A little weary in the afternoon — nearly dozed off, needed to go for a walk down the street to wake up," said Tommy.

"Well, guess what? I made contact with the clever Claire today. We are catching up for coffee tomorrow. You will never guess her excuse for calling me. She said the church needed some help with renewing some property leases."

"How very (dis)ingenuous," replied Tommy with more than a measure of sarcasm.

"Well, let's see how it plays out tomorrow. Anyway, I also wanted to tell you something else," said Jane with an uncertain hesitation as she paused.

"OK, what is it, Jane?" said Tommy, equally cautious.

"That week in Africa with you, well…it's done something to me. All day today, I missed not seeing you, not being able to reach out and know you were near. I just needed you to know that. And I have not felt that way about anyone for a long time."

Jane felt both relieved at finally communicating what had been building up inside but also exposed and nervous as to what Tommy's reply might be. The silent pause on the phone did not help and seemed to go on forever, but she knew she must not speak next if she wanted to bring Tommy into the open. Tommy finally and thankfully broke the silence.

"Jane, I know exactly what you mean. You know, I've felt the same way. But you are far braver than me at getting that out. I didn't want to disrespect the seriousness of these events that have brought us together, but you have increasingly occupied both my thoughts and my heart in a way that has taken me totally by surprise. Listen, I just got a call this afternoon, I have to be on the first plane into

Melbourne tomorrow morning and maybe for a few days, but I will call you tomorrow night yeah?"

"Oh, I see," said Jane, trying to hide her disappointment. "OK, that's fine, I will fill you in on the Claire chat then."

"Sure, and whatever you do, stay sweet with Claire and the church. I'm working on a plan that I will share with you when I get back. They have a global church conference coming up in the US. Hedgestone is the keynote speaker, of course, and all his crew will be there. I think you should go."

"What! Why would I want to do that?" said Jane. Tommy certainly managed to change the mood of the conversation.

"Don't worry. I've got an idea," Tommy assured her.

"Hmm, well I look forward to hearing more. You have a safe trip then; you better get an early night. Up at 4 am, I imagine?"

"Yes, I hate that flight, but it was either that or leave tonight, and I would have missed your call," said Tommy.

"Oh…really…well thank you for taking me into consideration for your travel plans, goodnight now."

"OK, talk tomorrow," said Tommy and hung up first.

Jane thought to herself, 'That could have gone a lot better.'

She had tried to get some feelings out, but Tommy was totally on-the-job-focused. Tiredness began to overtake her mind. It was a long first day back in the office. She took herself off to bed, turning her thoughts to a conversation plan with the ever clever and crafty Claire.

CHAPTER 19

CAFÉ OF DECEPTION

Arthur Hedgestone was the only person that ever seriously intimidated Claire Endor. His steely blue eyes knew no fear and could look straight through you without blinking. And when that gravelly gruff voice began to ask questions combined with the death stare, it felt like there was no escape. She prided herself on being the one that wielded the intimidation. But she realised she had met her match when she first met Hedgestone. That alignment of authority only deepened when she entered the employ of his church.

When she took the call from Hedgestone a few days ago, she knew that this was an important assignment and that she needed to deliver. What's more, Hedgestone knew that her marriage to Peter was an absolute sham. Peter had been up to no good for a long time. Claire had discovered Viagra in his business travel kit when helping him pack for a business trip a few years ago. Shock gave way to her native cunningness, and she put the pack of little blue pearls back where she found them – but not before counting them. On his return, she created an opportunity to search his bag before he unpacked and sure enough, three tablets were missing. The confrontation that followed was brutal and without mercy.

Peter had nowhere to go, no way of explaining why he needed to take Viagra on a business trip, let alone why was he taking it at all. Cornered and cowering like a beast before the slaughter, he fessed up everything, but not before laying the blame at Claire's feet for being a spiteful, ruthless witch that constantly belittled him in public. Of course, that was only fuel to Claire's flaming fury. They both knew that their marriage was a sham, but neither of them could let this become public knowledge. The very thought of the church vilification was too much to bear. Claire would almost certainly lose the position of influence and leadership that she had come to crave, with its elevated authority over others below her in the Hedgestone hierarchy. Peter would equally have to quit his role in the music ministry as a drummer.

The result – their lives became a total charade and mockery of the principles they had espoused every Sunday as one of the glam young couples of the young adults' ministry. Hedgestone didn't care for the state of their souls. He relished the thought that Claire had been added to his pool of people that would now do whatever he needed them to do to support his powerful position and help him maintain control over an organisation that now globally turned over $110 million a year.

Claire started her day with this full history bearing down on her, just as she did every other day. But today there was the chance to rebalance the power dynamics a little. If she could find out what Jane Johnson was up to and bring 'home the bacon' to Hedgestone, then maybe she could move forward in his favour and not live so nervously.

It was well before three pm when Claire found herself a discrete table for two in a quiet corner of the café. She had brought with her the lease papers to legitimise her meeting with Jane. It wasn't long before she spotted the light frame and elegantly dressed Jane making her way towards her.

"Claire, so wonderful to see you," said Jane, taking the lead as she approached the table.

"Hi, Jane, thanks for taking the time to catch up."

Claire caught the eye of the waiter and quickly ordered for both of them. "I wanted to see if you could assist us on this lease renewal for the main church facility in Hornsby. The landlord is putting in all these additional clauses for air conditioning maintenance and replacement before he will accept our renewal. I wondered if you could review the lease and the correspondence and provide us with some advice? Sorry I didn't realise you were away. Africa was it? How interesting?"

Jane deliberately did not respond to the Africa question. Jane continued to take the lead and control the conversation. She had set an exit door, hard finish to the meeting by arranging for Suzy to call her precisely at 3:40 pm to urgently return to the office, and was determined to burn as much time on her leading proceedings until then. "No problem at all. Just leave the documents with me, and I will come back to you early next week. Anyway, enough business, how have you been? Are you enjoying your ministry? How's Peter?"

Jane's last question caught her a little off guard. She tried not to show her discomfort. For an instant, Claire's fake smile froze as she glanced away and in that instant, gave away her pretence. Did Jane know about what Peter had been up to? She resumed her fake smiling defences, "Oh Peter is doing fine. We are both loving this season of life and ministry."

Jane picked up on Claire's uneasiness about the Peter question and tucked that away as future ammunition. Claire was not about to allow Jane any new access in that direction anyway. She immediately pressed again for the information she came for and was not about to leave empty-handed.

"So, Africa, such a short time, what did you get up to?" Claire quizzed again.

Jane was ready. "Claire, it is such an amazing place. I had forgotten just how beautiful it is there. You know I grew up there, right? And the people, such treasures. Their warmness and friendliness is so overwhelming, so refreshing for me personally. It's been 13 years since we left Maputo and do you know, I've never been back until last week? I just had this urge to get some closure on that whole chapter of our lives. I needed to visit my parents' grave. I can't even explain to you why but I've had this heaviness on my heart for so long recently. I have to tell you, I just bawled my eyes out. Lucky, I had a very supportive friend with me. Anyway, I caught up with lots of old acquaintances and realised — you know what, everybody has moved on and so have I. I mean, I'm always going to miss Mum and Dad, but I really got it that they died doing what they loved and achieved something very few people do — they did something incredibly significant for the Kingdom and touched so many lives throughout their ministry. How many of us get to do that?"

Jane drew breath and felt she had succeeded in telling the truth without sharing the truth she didn't need to share. And in doing so, truth carried her story to Claire with a transparency that gave Claire nothing with which to work.

"Yes, I've heard their ministry spoken of at leadership tables as the stuff of legends. You must be so proud of them?" said Claire, wanting to circle back to Jane's Africa activities. "Did you meet up with anyone else while you were there?"

This time, Jane found it difficult not to dilute true responses as she thought of her meetings with Sipho, Nathi and especially that Doeg. Nor did she want to reveal anything about Tommy's having accompanied her. Did Claire already know the answer to the question she was asking? Jane thought she did. Now was about when she wanted Suzy's exit call to interrupt.

"Just some old family friends," said Jane attempting to bat away any further inquiry. She felt vulnerable for a split second. "Do you mind if I quickly go to the bathroom?" she asked Claire and stood up to make her way to the ladies. Jane found herself a lavatory cubicle and closed the door to draw breath, and gather and calm her thoughts. After a few minutes, she went to the washbasin and looked at herself in the mirror to search for any giveaways in her countenance.

Claire had watched Jane make her move to the safety of the bathroom and knew only too well why Jane had retreated to that sanctuary, leaving her bag on the table. What woman goes to the bathroom and leaves her bag behind? She was well-versed in now or never strategies from her old life and, with one eye on the bathroom door, picked up her purse and fumbled through its contents. Gold! She found a security pass to 'Highview apartments' and quickly extracted it.

She saw the lady's bathroom door open out of the corner of her eye and quickly picked up her phone just before Jane made her way back, pretending to be text checking.

"And how is your father's old ministry church going. I hear it's still been growing all these years?" said Claire, with complete composure that concealed her actions.

Jane settled back into her chair and took on Claire's fixed gaze head-on without flinching. Everything in her wanted to blurt out what she had found out about Hedgestone and his persecution of her parents, but with great courage, she managed to restrain herself. That moment would surely come.

Finally, her phone buzzed with Suzie's text. She seized the interruption to proceedings with both hands, grabbing her cell phone, like an eagle its prey. "Oh, that's my four pm appointment. I had better make a move. Thank you so much for coming out to see me, Claire. Give me a week to work through the lease and those docs, and I will come back to you."

'Saved by the bell,' thought Claire. She was looking forward to going more in-depth. She needed to know more about what Jane had discovered regarding the death of her parents. All she was left with was a lot of uncertainty. Jane had given nothing away as to her possible knowledge of events. Claire was not happy. She knew Hedgestone would not be satisfied with uncertainty, and she did not look forward to reporting back to him. Before she could protest the end of their meeting, Jane was already on her feet and moving to the pay station to settle her account.

"OK, well, thank you, Jane. Speak with you soon," was all she could offer as she surrendered the meeting.

Jane pay-waved and exited without even turning back for a final acknowledgement. Job done.

Later that evening, Claire fronted up to reporting to Hedgestone directly. As she relayed the events of her afternoon's meeting with Jane, she was surprised that he did not come down on her a little heavier for not being able to come back with something more indicative of Jane's activities.

"Humph…" grumbled Hedgestone, "she's hiding things from you and knows something," he announced with an uncanny certainty and paused for a moment. "I gather you have not forgotten how to deal with a white rabbit, Claire? True love is sacrifice."

Claire was chilled to the core by Hedgestone's words and felt them enter her soul like a two-edged sword. She thought for a moment about how to answer. But then with unquestionable certainty and loyalty, she replied, "Not at all, Pastor Hedgestone, not at all," as she folded the security pass in her hands like a casino gambler holding an ace in his hands.

CHAPTER 20

INTEGRITY UNDERMINED

Dale and Dominique Johnson were a rare union of ministry friends. Although they were from amazingly different backgrounds — Dale, an ambitious commerce student that encountered a Damascus road conversion; and Dominique, the daughter of a devoted Presbyterian minister that grew up in an expectation of Christian commitment — both were inseparable from the time they first met at a creative ministry retreat.

Working together in music ministry created a platform for a friendship that grew into a whirlwind romance and later, marriage, which, in turn, grew into a family, that grew into an extended dedication to serve others with life-changing principles of the gospel they had so successfully applied to their own lives. Importantly, they had both made up their minds that they wanted to make their lives count for more than a house, a mortgage, 2.7 children and retirement at 66 years of age. Therein lay the great strength of their relationship. It was not a case of Dale dragging a dominated Dominique to the mission field and her abiding because it was her duty to support her husband. Instead, she had made up her mind, in the reality of her own calling, that this is what she wanted to do with all the breath of her days. If Dale was ever down and struggling for ongoing direction, Dominque was there to remind him of the call, the cause and their mutual consecration. If Dom was ever having a bad day and dreaming of the white sandy beaches of Bondi or the endless shopping malls of Chatswood, rather than the open sewer channels that winded their way through African squatter camps,

Dale could equally apply correction to toughen up princess and speak into her life a remembrance of the eternal value of a single soul.

Side by side, they supported each other, knowingly navigating the spiritual landscape that was their Mozambican mission in Maputo. This was the capstone of all of their ministry training and previous ministry endeavours in Australia. This was the opportunity to apply all they had learnt and become, to a mission field that was truly ripe for harvest. And they loved every minute of it. So many responded to the simple call of salvation, so many dramatic and authentic life conversions. This was a time of perfect convergence of the Johnson's position in life ministry and groups of people who were eager for change and a genuine faith community experience. Dale and Dom connected thousands to the reality of a loving saviour that could bring real change into their lives. Relentlessly, they outreached to the poorest of the poor, to students in high schools with open opportunity to address school assemblies, to lives bound in the fear and domination of tribal witchcraft with its muti and ancestral observances. And the fruit was amazing and long-lasting. Church services multiplied from a single service on a Sunday to two services, then to four every Sunday with two in the morning and two in the evening. Midweek cottage meetings sprung up all over town as leaders were trained, ready to deliver togetherness in simple gatherings in over 40 locations every midweek.

Within two years, the Johnsons had built up the fastest-growing congregation anywhere in the Africa collective of the Gospel Outreach Fellowship of churches. They were directly touching over 3,000 people a week and finances were built with free will giving that enabled the work to become financially self-supporting — something not often achieved in Mozambique.

Hedgestone had watched all of this from a distance with a quiet ambition to seize his moment and keep the labours and enterprise of the Johnsons work but remove them as its leaders. He never liked Johnson. He was young, radical and used his methods and ministry model, setting aside the Hedgestone 'pattern' of doing things. Hedgestone did not mind ministers not using his methods — so long as they miserably failed so that he could use them as examples in conference messages to reinforce that his methods were God-given and the 'only pattern'.

But not so Johnson. He was successful. And now others were asking him what he was doing and how was he doing it. Johnson was only too eager to help and share what was working for him, much to the angst of Hedgestone.

Always the strategist, Hedgestone began to make his move by isolating any pastor that showed an interest or expressed praise for what the Johnsons were doing. They were withdrawn from any preaching opportunities at local or international conferences where they might gain influence. If they were African missionaries relying on funding, then he issued instructions that their funding be cut to zero over six months, leaving them to fend for themselves in a foreign country where visas restricted employment opportunities. He publicly ridiculed and belittled their efforts with very thinly veiled references in regular leadership forums. Everyone knew who he was talking about. He was the absolute master at creating a culture of shunning and ousting those he had marked.

He did not take on Johnson directly. He slowly but surely first undermined any support lines he had and then began extinguishing any influence he had within the Fellowship. Johnson began to get phone calls and visits from ministry friends and colleagues, not knowing what to do as Hedgestone relentlessly undermined their ministry and made it impossible for them to continue. He often sent in new pastoral leadership on a Sunday to take over churches, literally forcing the resignation of the incumbent as their work visas were cancelled. They could no longer endure the personal assaults upon their families and calling. Others were called in to 'leadership tribunal' forums where they were cross-examined and subjected to the harshest of controlling judgments. Then they were told that their ministry was no longer endorsed by Hedgestone. Having often invested a great deal of their finances into their ministries, not to mention the sacrifices made by their families in relocating to second and third world economies, they were told to pack their bags and be gone before the next Sunday. They were often threatened with legal action if they dared to discuss their circumstances with anyone, including their congregations or church elderships. Hedgestone had already lined up new ministry teams to take over their churches and finances. These hirelings called church meetings and presented a tirade of lies and fabricated smears against the former pastors. Every conceivable allegation was made as to unacceptable behaviour in morals and money, all completely fabricated and unsubstantiated. The charge of 'disloyalty to headship' always made an appearance.

Dale Johnson was no fool, and neither was his wife, Dom. They could see the destruction Hedgestone was dishing out and he wept with many of their friends at the callous and calculated actions they endured as the purge continued. He knew it was only a matter of time before Hedgestone would come after him. There was no way he was about to let Hedgestone destroy all the work that they had done. Strategically and respectfully, he progressively wrote to Hedgestone and the church fellowship board of elders for clarification regarding their actions, purposes and future intentions.

Hedgestone welcomed the engagement. He knew Johnson would have no choice but to make a move towards him. Johnson's congregation was very large, the largest of all the churches in southern Africa, as was the church income base. He would need to be strategic if he wished to remove Johnson but avoid a church split and retain as much of the congregation and income base as he could. Hedgestone replied to Johnson's letters with great brevity, refraining from commenting in writing on the issues raised and reminding him frequently that if he felt fatigued or unable to continue in his role or function in the context of fellowship guidelines, then a replacement would be made available to continue the work and his extraction would be facilitated.

Next, Hedgestone began to plant local operatives from other churches into Johnson's church, like Dobbie Doeg. They were given instructions to be disruptive and draw congregation support away from Dale Johnson, to challenge Johnson and call him out at council meetings on any action or word that could be interpreted as disloyal towards Hedgestone.

Finally, Dale and Dom came to the conclusion that they could no longer continue under the increasingly controlling and threatening influence that emanated from the leadership of Hedgestone. They knew that if they wanted to continue to reach the souls of the desperate and hurting, then they could not compromise their liberty or obedience to fundamental principles of the Gospel endeavour. If Hedgestone gained control of their work, they knew the momentum would swing in the opposite direction, from souls to a dominating personality cult where money generation and flow back to Hedgestone, away from the local community, was the priority. They knew something had shifted deep within their souls: the enthusiasm that had so swept up their lives towards focused sacrifice for their fellow souls and an eternal perspective governing all their life pursuits, was gone. Something that was once alive with the breath of the Holy Spirit had turned into a stone-cold monolith — a memorial to one man's greed and manipulation, where personal 'gold' giftings were transformed into devices for domination and the destruction of people's lives and ministries. Hedgestone had turned and looked back, wondering what was in it for him and in that moment, had become monumentally pillarized with all the reality of Lot's wife. His flesh moved on, but his spirit was frozen dead in the moment, his gaze transfixed upon a carnal city construct of man's indulgence in life without the Spirit of God, already marked for destruction.

Dale and Dom were always taught to use the gold but don't touch the glory; to be pilgrims, and not proprietors; to serve others, and not seek to be served. Once there had been a cause — a purpose — but Hedgestone had chosen to become his own cause. A cause to create a personal dynasty that controlled others with an iron fist but removed all accountability when it came to his own conduct.

Together with their ministry team led by Sipho, Dale and Dom had decided what they must do. Rather than be labelled as deceitful or disloyal, they would draft one final letter of intention to Hedgestone. No more questions about clarification or appeals for an explanation. They would inform him that as an individual local church, they had decided that they would seek their own determination and cease all formal accountability and association with Hedgestone and his Global Outreach Fellowship. Unfortunately, this was a letter that Dale Johnson never got to write.

CHAPTER 21

MARRIAGE AND MINISTRY

It was a beautiful African morning when Dale rose early for his devotions. The sun edged over the horizon and the birds began their raucous morning chatter, as only African birdlife can. Although he had kept this discipline for nearly 20 years, he did so with all the earnest desperation of the hour, his voice free of mindless religious repetition.

Prayer life was incredibly important to Dale. Not because someone had told him to do it, or as a way to set an example for others, but because it was the very lifeblood of his ministry. He could no more function without it then he could live without water. This was the meeting place where he daily built and checked his defences against the distractions and deceptions of the enemy. It was the place where he uplifted Dominique, Jane and Paul before the Lord for their protection and His presence in their hearts, to keep and prosper. He moved forward from his blood kin to his church family, naming them and bringing them also before the Lord as their faces emerged before him, and he sought to look into their hearts and identify their needs. For this city, Maputo, and this war-ravaged, abused and corrupted nation had become as dear to him as his beloved Australia.

Finally, silence overtook his spoken prayers, and he submitted himself to it, searching his own heart for signs of the enemy. Then, once the demands of the day began to creep into his thoughts, he focused his attention on getting through 3 Psalms and a chapter of Proverbs. He had always been a slow reader and took his time, often re-reading to see if he had missed a cadence or connection. He knew when he was done.

Dale called out to Dom as he moved from his study to the kitchen to check if his coffee machine was ready to help kickstart the day.

"Hey Dom, are you ready? Coffee is on, and we need to get an early start for Nelspruit."

"Hang on. You know I need to organise the kids before we go," said Dom, allowing her voice to echo and bounce off the walls from the bedroom with just the right volume to gently remind her husband of something that he should already know by now — that she wouldn't be rushed whenever they were preparing to go out. She made her way to her daughter's bedroom, checking in on her son Paul on the way, who was, as expected, still deeply in slumberland. Dom smiled and closed the door. Her children had grown up too quickly, but the African experience provided an excellent environment for them all to come together with an intra-dependent closeness they might never have had in Sydney.

"Jane, honey, Dad and I are doing a day trip down to Nelspruit and will be back late this afternoon. If we are late, don't worry, Grace is here all day, and I've made pasta on the stove."

"OK, Mum. Are you taking Paul with you?" asked Jane, hoping to have the house, and the computer and internet, all to herself.

"No, he is still sleeping. You look after your brother, please. I don't want to hear of any tantrums or petty disputes from Grace when I get back," said Dom.

Jane put her pillow over her head and let out a silent scream. Paul could be so irritating when her parents weren't around.

"I heard that Jane," Dom said as she made her way to the kitchen. She knew her children only too well. With Jane in the middle of her teenage years and Paul on the verge of his, she continually had all her sensors out, ready to head off any possible disputes between them that might be emerging on the horizon.

"And get some studying done, please. You've got exams next week, remember." Dom had picked up long ago that Jane had inherited her father's intellect and analytical mind. She had identified significant potential in Jane. However, she did have a tendency to be a little lazy from time to time and take things for granted. Both her children were enrolled in an international school with an excellent academic standard, but Dom was not going to leave their education to them alone and closely monitored their progress and performance.

"Your coffee is on the table, honey," said Dale, glad that Dom had surfaced and keen to make sure his call for her readiness had not put him too offside.

"Thank you, dear," said Dom assuredly, letting him know he was not in the doghouse and the three-hour drive would not be one that forced him to endure an Icelandic climate.

Dale had the 4-wheel drive running and ready. He really enjoyed these once-a-month road trips. It was not only a chance for them both to get out of town and enjoy some of the niceties of South Africa not readily available in Maputo, as well as pick up some foodie favourites for the kids, but it was also a chance to spend some alone time with Dom and do an 'is-everything-ok with-you?' relationship audit with his wife. He was very conscious of the sacrifice he had called on his family to make. Living in a developing economy when they could have a lot more creature comforts in Sydney was ever-present in his thoughts. He always wanted to reassure himself that he was not expensing their lives in the pursuit of his own calling. This was a family consecration, and it was his job to make sure they were emotionally cashed-up for the journey.

Jane jumped in the car and positioned her coffee travel mug, found her sunglasses in the glovebox and settled in for the journey.

"7:25 am, and we're on the road — that's a great effort, missy," said Dale.

"Of course, and if you hadn't commenced romantic interludes at 6 am this morning, we would have been on the road at 7," commented Dom with a sly smile that banked some emotional capital for the journey.

Dale laughed, "I am truly a richly blessed man and thank the Lord for you every day!"

The golden glaze of the early morning eastern sunrise filled the cabin from behind them. Both of them had learnt to love the early morning and late evening low horizon African sun. Conversation seemed unnecessary between them — it would have only served to spoil and almost disrespect the moment. It was 30kms later before they resumed their chat.

"You have to help keep Jane focused on her studies, Dale," said Dom as her thoughts for Jane's future erupted into a request for Dale's assistance.

"We may not always be here, and when we get back to Australia, she needs to be in a position where she can pursue tertiary study. She is a very bright girl and a deep thinker. Sometimes when she expresses her thoughts, she demonstrates an amazing vocabulary and economy of words — just a great communicator. We need to cultivate and help develop those skills."

"Ah, she is fine. You worry too much. But I know what you mean. Jane and I have some great chats one-on-one when she comes with me to the orphanages around town. I stir up her gift and get that little head and heart working. She already has that momentum going, and nothing you or I do will stop it. It's Paul we need to be conscious of. He lives in his sister's shadow and is so dependent on her — more than he likes to admit. He is definitely the sensitive one and doesn't yet have his sister's emotional confidence."

'Paul, my baby boy...' thought Dom. "It's true, he is very dependent on her."

"You have to know when to be there and when not to be. He wants to move on from being your 'baby boy.' You have to create some space for him to do that. But it's all good. I've got him covered and know where he is at. I've got some man time planned away with him soon, maybe we'll get across to Victoria Falls for a weekend".

Dom was reminded just why she loved this man so much. He was always so 'pro-visionary' for his family, always looking out for their 'next.' Not only a provider but always consciously planning for their provision, both emotionally and spiritually. And that alone created a climate of security and contentment that was extraordinarily comforting in so many ways. She could not think of anything she wanted for, or anything that was lacking in her life. When she ministered to her church at young women's events, this family covering and its value permeated and penetrated all her teaching. It was precious gold, and the young girls caught it. They wanted what she had. They silently observed and soaked up all the unspoken nuances of watching their pastor and his wife interact with so much love and affection, playfulness and tenderness, full of respect and dignity. The power of Dom's testimony, lived out daily amongst them, was incredibly effective — beyond what Dom or Dale could ever calculate. In a culturally immoral environment where almost anything went in terms of relationships, and all the resulting fallout — the callous destruction of the AIDS epidemic and fatherless homes — Dom's work enabled a young generation to make moral choices that would bless their own lives forever. It virtually changed the history of their communities as these young women reset the moral climate and turned the tide of cultural abuse.

Dale broke into her thoughts with his own reflections. "You know I was reading 1 Samuel this week — you know, chapter 7, vs 12 where Samuel sets the Ebenezer stone and sets a landmark in both place and time, as the enemy of Israel is turned back upon itself, and he catches the moment and says, *Thus far the Lord has helped us.* Just amazing! I was thinking of us, how God has helped us so much, blessed our family, blessed our church. God has been so good to us! Samuel realises and acknowledges the powerful intervention and involvement in their lives, sets the stone, acknowledges who He is. To all Israel, he says 'Let's remember this moment and this place.'"

Dom reached out her hand and put in on his thigh, gently squeezing it. "Yes, it's amazing Dale. I'm so glad we made the decision to be here and do what we've done. And Hedgestone and his cronies will never take that away from us."

Dale's thankfulness for a wife like Dom was interrupted as he took a concealed bend in the highway. "What's that up ahead?" he asked.

There was something on the road. It looked like a large truck manifold, completely obstructing their way. Dale was an excellent driver and knew he had to avoid hitting it at all costs. He slammed on the brakes and swerved into a clearing just off the road, as he instinctively put out his hand across Dom's chest.

"Are you all right, Dom?"

But before she could answer, the car was surrounded by young men screaming and guns pointing at them.

"Get out of the car, get out of the car now!" yelled one young man, who appeared to be their leader.

"OK, OK," said Dale. "Calm down, calm down, you can have the car."

"Don't tell us to calm down. Get out now!" the man insisted, with lips quivering and what seemed to be as much fear in his eyes as in Dale's.

Dom lifted her hands high where they could see them and began to pray silently. Dale, always the soul winner, looked into the man's eyes and could see that this was no hardened criminal.

"You don't have to do this. There is a better way than this. Let me give you something," said Dale, with all the calming compassion he could find. He reached into the glove box to get a salvation tract he often kept in there for impromptu sharing opportunities.

"He's getting a gun, he's getting a gun!" yelled another of their crew.

"Shoot him, quickly!" he yelled. Before Dom or Dale could say another word, the guns opened fire all around the car. Round after round was fired until no one inside the vehicle was moving at all.

Dale had tried to cover and protect Dom, but it was too late. Her body fell into his arms as her eyes looked into his. They both knew this was the end. "I love you, Dale...the children..." were the last words he heard, as they both passed into eternity from the multiple gunshot words that hit them.

The hijackers were stunned. One, in particular, was screaming at them. "Why did you shoot? Why? You weren't supposed to hurt them, just steal the car!". He wandered around in circles, gun still in his hand. "What are we going to do now? What are we going to do?"

Another of the gang stepped forward and took charge. "Shut up Nathi. Just shut your mouth." Get their bodies out of there now.

Take the car back to the chop shop. Let's get out of here before someone sees us."

They quickly dragged Dom and Dale out of the car and left their bodies by the side of the road. Masked weaver birds went back to their business in the trees above as the heat of the African sun began to dry the blood that drained from Dale and Dom's bodies, as it mixed into the red earth beneath them.

CHAPTER 22

A TRAIL OF DECEIT DISCOVERED

Jane awoke from a deep sleep very slowly. Her mind began to recall pieces of her exchange with Claire Endor the previous day. She had not connected at all that she was missing her backup security apartment pass that she kept in her purse, as she always used the key tag pass she kept on her car keyring.

She habitually reached for her phone. Nothing from Tommy — not a text or a voice message since last night after she crashed early. A disappointed frown and pursed lips broke across her countenance. She secretly thought to herself that Tommy would have — should have — wanted to know how her day had transpired, and she needed to know what he was planning for this GoF conference. She decided to text him.

"Hey, are phones still working in your part of the country? Give me a call."

Jane took herself off to the shower and got ready for the day. It was only when she was packing her bag that she came across the envelope with the lease papers that Claire had given her as a pretence for assistance to prompt the meeting. She opened the envelope and began to work through the documents. A letter from the landlord to Ministry Management Pty Ltd and a copy of the original lease for the church premises. The letter simply detailed some make good provisions in the lease contract concerning repairs and building equipment maintenance. Nothing unusual there. Jane thought to herself. She made herself a coffee and began to cross-reference the relevant lease clauses. All of the landlord's requests seemed to be in order.

It wasn't until she was on the train to the office that her inquisitive mind began to interrogate and agitate the name of the tenant in those documents. 'Ministry Management? Who is that?' As soon as she got to the office, she found one of her assistants in the kitchen, making himself a coffee.

"Hey Charlie, can you do something for me?"

"Sure, Jane, what do you need?" replied the first-year graduate.

"I need you to do a company search on Ministry Management Pty Ltd and cross-reference everything you find with Global Outreach Fellowship of Australia Incorporated. See if you can download their annual report from their website. Get it to me before lunch, please Charlie. Also, see if you can draft me a response to this landlord for notice of a lease renewal," said Jane as she handed Charlie Claire's envelope of documents.

"OK, will do," said Charlie, feeling the urgency in Jane's voice and wanting to please his senior partner.

"Good man, Charlie," said Jane over her shoulder as she made her way to her office. Claire may have carelessly opened the door to something that didn't quite make sense and Jane was at her best in these situations. Just a whiff of something that seemed inconsistent and she relentlessly turned her vibrant mind to the trail. Why was the tenant of the property 'Ministry Management' and not the church incorporated association that operated the church ministry? She knew something of human nature that others often passed over. People did things for a reason. Nothing ever failed to make sense. There was a reason, and she was going to find out what that was.

The transforming crucibles of life events that Jane was forced to deal with as a 16-year-old girl suddenly without parents and having to care for her younger brother had given her a unique and rare ability in her perception of human behaviour and its innate ability to deceive and obscure its actions. Piecing together people's guilt and motives was a challenge that she embraced with great tenacity.

A few hours later, Charlie appeared in the door of her office.

"OK, I've got something for you, Jane," said Charlie with a grin from ear to ear (and if he had had a tail, it would have been wagging from side to side with great excitement.)

"That was quick! Come in. Close the door. Let's have a look at what you've got," said Jane.

"Ministry Management has a sole company director and secretary, an Arthur Othello Hedgestone of Arizona, USA, and a single shareholder, Temple Investments Inc, of the same registered address," said Charles, pausing for breath.

"Go on," enticed Jane.

"Now, this is interesting. The lease is for the rent and outgoings of $385,000 per annum but the rent paid in the annual report under property outgoings is $462,000 per annum," said Charlie with a checkmate bravado.

"So, what we are seeing is that Hedgestone has put in place an intermediary that he controls which, in turn, subleases the property to the church for a hidden markup of $77,000 per year. That's a nice mark-up for doing nothing. A small conflict of interest, don't you think?"

"Classic skimming scam might be the blunter interpretation of that transaction," said Charlie.

"OK, I tell you what I want you to do now," said Jane decisively, knowing this was a significant trail alert and one she was not about to pass by. "Drill down further into their accounts. Public utilities, government rates and taxes, airfares, speaking engagements, fees — make schedules for all of them as to the amount claimed in the accounts, and let's see what external substantiation we can get. He is likely to be passing everything through his 'Ministry Management' company at a markup on costs."

"OK, OK, but to whom do I book this time? Do we have an engagement for this?" said Charlie.

"Just book it to…book it to…Hedgestone Monuments," said Jane, creatively raising a case matter entry on the fly that would at least keep Charlie moving, even though she actually had no engagement to book work to.

Jane stood up quickly and grabbed her handbag to head out for a coffee. She was not about to hang around for any further probing questions from Charlie. Exiting the building, she found herself a quiet spot on a park bench and rang Tommy's mobile. Tommy still had not called or texted her, but she felt he needed to know of these latest developments.

"Hello, Jane?" said Tommy inquiringly.

"Tommy!" said Jane, with a genuine gladness just to hear his voice. "Hey, are you still in Melbourne?"

"Yes but good news — I'm coming back early tonight. I should be back by 8.30."

"OK, great. I've got some interesting stuff I want to go over with you. Why don't you call by my place on the way home? I'll have some dinner ready for you. Don't eat anything on the plane," said Jane, taking advantage of Tommy's new schedule.

"I will def look forward to that!" said Tommy. "But tell me more — what have you been up to?"

"Well, I was simply doing some inquiries to draft a response for Claire's questions on the lease renewal, and you won't believe what I found," said Jane, like a cat with a mouse.

"Go on," said Tommy.

"I'll tell you tonight. Gotta go. See you soon," said Jane, knowingly adding a double incentive for Tommy to drop by her place: food and information. What man could refuse that?

"But, Ja…" was all Tommy could get out before Jane had terminated the call.

Jane's mind went into overdrive. This was when she was at her best. She began to run two strategies in parallel. One, to get some alone time with Tommy, whom she increasingly found herself wanting to be with; and secondly, how to build and present a position that exposed Hedgestone. It had been quite a while since Jane had felt this motivated, and the adrenalin of expectancy was pulsating strongly through her veins. Quite pleased with herself, she made her way back to the office, planning a dinner menu that might impress Tommy.

CHAPTER 23

ROMANCE AND REVELATIONS

Tommy succeeded in getting a 45-minute snap nap on the flight back from Melbourne, interrupted only by the steward's announcements for landing preparations. He slowly came to his senses, feeling decidedly better for getting some timely shut-eye, as he had been on the go since five-thirty am. He checked his watch, and it was moving onto ten past eight. With only carry-on luggage, he thought he should be in his car and on the road to Jane's by eight forty pm.

Again, he wondered to himself what Jane might have discovered. She certainly enjoyed taunting and teasing him from time to time, Tommy reflected. He found her playfulness quite romantically engaging and was certainly looking forward to dinner together. Their schedules had both been quite hectic since they got back from Africa. Tonight would provide an excellent opportunity to reconnect.

While Tommy's plane was circling Mascot Airport for what seemed like the umpteenth time, Jane was putting the final touches to her spaghetti aioli, a concoction she thought might appeal to Tommy's southern European background. Finely chopped broccolini heads with pan-fried sopressa salami, drenched in virgin olive oil infused with garlic and basil, tossed with al dente pasta and plenty of egg yolk and beaten with grated romano cheese, had to impress any hungry young man. Especially when accompanied by an aromatic pinot noir. Plus, of course, her presence. She had a quick taste of the pasta and decided it needed one more dosing of olive oil, before a quick toss and turn, and then back on with the lid, simmering on the lowest of heat.

The table was set, the ciabatta bread warm from the oven, and the wine open. All Jane needed was for the doorbell to ring in the next ten minutes. Time to get ready.

She wanted to get out of her work clothes into something more relaxed and did not want this to look like a client meeting. But she also did not want to be too casual or flirtatiously interpreted, although secretly she did want to inspire attention. She quickly reconciled her competing intentions and chose wisely from her extensive wardrobe when she heard her phone buzz from an incoming text.

Yes, it was Tommy: "In the car, on the road, very hungry..." he wrote. Followed by a toothy smiling face.

'OK,' she thought, 'he is still likely at least ten minutes away.' Time to cut the heat from her pasta and let it rest. Jane hoped Tommy was not going to be too much longer or her best culinary efforts would start to go gluey.

'Music!' thought Jane. More choices. She went with her Miles Davis, *Kinda Blue* CD. Very relaxed, without romantic overtones and undisputed musicianship from Miles.

Tommy plied his way through fortunately light traffic and found a very convenient car parking spot outside Jane's apartment. As he walked to the entrance, he was quietly excited to catch up with Jane and did not notice the shadowy figure sitting quite discreetly in the car across the street. Tommy made his way to Jane's door and rang the doorbell. The 'dong' of the ding-dong had barely finished before Jane was standing before him with the most welcome of smiles. He noticed instantly that she had gone to some trouble for the evening, with her long mouse blond hair partially done up in a bun, but still falling over the most gorgeous satin white blouse, loosely buttoned. The aroma of sorpressa salami, garlic and olive oil lingered behind her.

"Hi!" greeted Jane and leaned in for the briefest of cheek kisses. "Come in, so good to see you."

Tommy breathed in just a hint of Jane's Chanel No.5 as she withdrew from him. He quickly stepped inside.

"Something smells great! I hope you have not gone to too much trouble? You know you don't have to keep secrets from me to get me to come over for dinner right?" said Tommy, letting Jane know that she was not the only strategically-trained lawyer in the room.

"Oh, don't be daft!" objected Jane, pouring a red and putting the glass in Tommy's hand without asking. "Come and sit down. You must be exhausted from your busy schedule and flight from Melbourne."

"Wow, you are looking fantastic! And something smells deliciously like my mother's cooking. You haven't been talking to her, have you?"

"Do you seriously think I would need to ring your mother to put this together? This is just leftovers from last night — sorry to disappoint you — too busy for anything else."

"I don't believe you for one-minute, Ms Johnson. Lawyers should know how to lie better than that!"

Jane laughed off his comments and retreated from making any further denials of intention.

"Anyway, while you've been earning the big bucks down in Melbourne, my team and I have been doing some valuable research." Jane picked up Tommy's plate and elegantly twirled a pasta serving for him and then did her own.

"That's what I came here for! I mean, to hear about your valuable research…and this beautiful pasta," said Tommy, equally delicately trying to balance both offerings.

"That's very good," added Tommy as he took his first fork of pasta.

"You should wait for the parmesan," said Jane, standing over Tommy's plate and showering it with grated fresh cheese.

Tommy withdrew from his second mouthful and sat extremely still as he could not help noticing the proximity of Jane's well-rounded bosom so close to his face, bouncing as she grated.

"Oops, sorry!" Tommy excused himself, "I was just so hungry, and it smelled so good."

Jane sat down. "Anyway, look at this!" she said as she dropped Charlie's tabulated spreadsheet in front of him.

Tommy reached for his wine with one hand and picked up the report with the other. "What's this?"

"Rent, electricity, rates and taxes, maintenance, property outgoings and more — all paid out from the incorporated church association to an offshore intermediary company controlled by Hedgestone and then back to the original landlord or other suppliers." Jane was moving early into full flight but paused for pasta bites as Tommy's eyes ran down the page to the totals.

"What? And so, the total margin between the source service provider and the church expense is $87,540? OK, this is big!" said Tommy.

"And that's just the last financial year. He's been doing it for years. And that's not including his annual speaking engagements here. Hedgestone gets a $10,000 per night speaking fee. Right, now multiply that by how many churches across GOF? 2,540 at last count? We are talking major, major skimming and diversion of funds. I think these practices were what so disturbed my father."

"No wonder he is so controlling and hellbent on removing any objectors to his methods or anyone who might question his authority," said Tommy. "There is no way he could allow folks like your parents to create any movement or momentum to resist him."

Tommy put the report down and got back to eating. "This is delicious. I was not aware of just how far your talents extended."

"Well, hang around, and you just might find out, Tommy," said Jane with an invitational smile and directness that made Tommy's blood rush. "OK, so what do we do with this?"

"You know, if this legal thing doesn't work out for you, you should seriously consider opening an Italian restaurant," said Tommy, swirling and scoffing forkfuls of spaghetti.

"Can you focus for a minute?! I've put hours into this. And it's not very attractive when you talk and eat at the same time," protested Jane.

"Sorry, Jane," said Tommy without pausing between mouthfuls. Jane glared at him.

"No seriously," said Tommy, putting his fork down with a particular emphasis. "This is great stuff — I mean your work with Charlie. If we have decided that the name of the game is to shame and blame Hedgestone and set aside for the moment what that monster did to your family, then you need to keep digging, because this fits in with the master plan I've been thinking about."

"Yes, what was that idea of yours you were telling me about? Some conference coming up?"

"Here's the thing, Jane. Hedgestone prides himself on 'discipleship' methods, and mantra's that he is following. What he says is a biblical pattern of effectively raising a Christian 'master race,' so that he has the ability to reproduce himself in others and in doing so, trigger an evangelical multiplication process that is way beyond himself in terms of reach and depth. That's how he built his 2,500 plus church network across the globe. There is one small problem, though. When Jesus did it, he was reproducing something holy and righteous and loving and deeply spiritual in others. When Hedgestone does it, he only breeds corruption and manipulation and nepotism because that's who he has become. You can only reproduce after your own DNA. Underneath the wafer-thin veneer of gospel rhetoric are a dead man's bones. Look at this report you've given me — it's corruption by any interpretation."

Tommy paused only to delight himself in the red pinot noir. "I have to tell you — you've matched the wine superbly with your pasta. We have to do this again."

'He is definitely a foodie,' noted Jane.

"So here is what we have to do," continued Tommy. "We need to create a forum where he is judged by his own first, and then the authorities. Let his disciples judge him, which is effectively being judged by yourself in his world. Then, when we have removed the platform of support he so desperately relies upon, we bring in the authorities and let that play out as it should. But here is the beautiful part of all of this: We don't need to create the forum — he does it himself. Every year in the States, he holds a mega 8,000 plus people discipleship conference event. He calls back the leadership groups from all over the world and then every night for a week, he reloads and tightens the bolts and makes sure his ship is in good shape for another year."

Jane had been digesting his words and his plan far better than Tommy had her pasta. "You shouldn't eat so quickly. Good Italian food always needs to be savoured slowly and thoughtfully. Otherwise, you miss all of the flavours working together. Anyway, I like your plan. But it's a little light on the detail. Do you think he is going to welcome you on stage to do a PowerPoint presentation?"

Tommy smiled across the table. "Ye of little faith, Jane! Indeed, I'm still working out the details, and that's where I need your help and maybe the help of your brother Paul."

"Paul? How could he be involved," said Jane with a great deal of spontaneous enthusiasm.

For the next hour, Tommy went through all of the details of what he had worked out so far. Back and forth they went, feeding off each other's ideas. Weaving together their thoughts into a fabric that materialised into a blueprint before them. Designing, creating, reinforcing and cross-checking each other. The clocked ticked later and later, and they only paused when the pinot bottle had given up its last drop.

Finally, when they had talked themselves out of huff and puff, Tommy found himself awkwardly looking into Jane's eyes for longer than was acceptable, and then down at the empty plates, considering whether he had outstayed his invitation.

"Wow, it's getting onto midnight. That was an amazing meal. Can I help you with the dishes?" offered Tommy, thinking that might be fun.

"No, no, you better get going. You must be so tired after the flight and your late nights in Melbourne," said Jane, standing up.

"Are you sure? OK, I will get going." Tommy stood up and followed Jane to the front door of her apartment.

"I'll walk you down," said Jane, not wanting things to get awkward but also wanting to let Tommy know that she wanted to move the relationship forward between them.

Jane paused at the front entrance to the street and decided that she would be the one to communicate something beyond their growing friendship of recent weeks.

Just as Tommy was about to reach for the door handle, Jane grabbed his hand.

"Wait, Tommy," she said, with a most careful and subtle emotion in her voice.

Jane then lifted her left hand behind Tommy's head and without warning, closed her eyes and gently and softly kissed Tommy with a press and hold for precisely the right measure of time, that let Tommy know some of the intent of her heart.

Tommy reacted without hesitation, embracing Jane and pulling her in closer, and making sure she knew he was kissing her back. Jane pulled back first and looked into Tommy's dark and dreamy eyes.

"I enjoyed tonight very much," said Jane.

Tommy looked back at Jane, and a thousand thoughts ran through his head with the kiss still fresh on his lips. "It was great to catch up. Next time, you let me cook something for you," he said.

"I look forward to it," said Jane, knowing she had to break the embrace. "You're welcome to cook in my kitchen anytime."

Tommy smiled right back at Jane, as he digested what that invitation might mean, before making his way through the door and into the night.

Across the street sitting in the car, Claire Endor's wait had been worth her while. She snapped the photos of Tommy and Jane's embrace at the door and zoomed in for multiple shots of their faces. 'Who is this guy?' she thought to herself. She waited until Tommy's car had pulled out in front of her before entering the traffic at a safe distance behind his vehicle. She might very well have something to report to Hedgestone in the morning.

CHAPTER 24

WITCHES AND WARLOCKS

Claire Endor always enjoyed her day off from church office duties for several reasons, not least her indulgence in obscurity with her personal trainer at a health club on the other side of town, where there was very little likelihood of her bumping into anyone from church circles. It was her time to be another person — away from what she considered the burden of having to live out this expected church behaviour and testimony. She could step into her old self-life, without Peter, without religious observance, even if it were just for a day.

She packed her gym kit, complete with a change of clothes and was in her car by ten am. She felt good about herself as she sped down the highway. Her Calvin Klein *Obsession* fragrance filled the car cabin, her new leotards and workout wear hugged her fit body in all the right places, and it would not be long before she had some solo time with Patrick at the gym.

Besides all of that, she had a good report to bring Hedgestone in her conference call scheduled for later that night. Her surveillance of Jane's apartment had paid off. Having followed Tommy's car home and then raided his letterbox the next day, she finally had a name: Tommy Cacao. She had already worked out that this was likely the guy Doeg had seen with Jane in Africa, and now he was making late-night visits to her home.

Jane's story didn't line up. Visiting friends in Africa? Really? Jane and Tommy, both lawyers, both on a mysterious short turnaround trip to Africa, Jane being very defensive and evasive at their coffee catchup meeting – something didn't add up.

'Hedgestone was right,' she thought. Nothing unusual there. Jane was up to something. Why was it so important to Hedgestone to know about the Africa trip?

Claire pulled up at the gym and made the entrance she loved to make, loud and noticed by everyone else nearby as she almost cat walked to the sign-in counter.

"Hi Trudi," she greeted the receptionist behind the desk as she signed in. "You have got me booked in for 10:45 with Personal Trainer, Patrick, right?"

"Yep, sure. Patrick has you permanently booked every Monday," the young receptionist assured Claire.

Claire quickly dropped her bag into her locker and made her way across the gym floor with her eyes scanning the machine stations for Patrick. Finally, she sighted him on the treadmill.

"Oh, so you thought you would start without me? You know I'm paying for this session?" Claire took Patrick by surprise, and he immediately halted the treadmill when he heard her voice behind him.

"Hey Claire, you know I need to get my heart going before I can take you on," Patrick hit back.

Claire looked Patrick up and down and admired again the chunky deltoids rising out of Patrick's shoulders, supported by the well-defined lats and triceps. "Well, I hope you can keep up with me, or I will need to find me something younger and fitter," Claire taunted.

"Enough talking, start working. Go warm up and find me in the free weights area. We will see who keeps up with who," said Patrick, taking back some authority.

Claire jumped on a bike and watched her Adonis complete his warm-up with some lightweight repetitions. It wasn't long before he was spotting her, as Claire pushed through some incline chest presses. Patrick stood behind her and gently supported her elbows and arms. Softly he whispered into her ear, "Make sure you breath when you push. How long do you have today?"

"I've got the whole afternoon. And you?"

"Until three this afternoon" replied Patrick. "You know I can't wait to be with you."

Claire smiled to herself. Patrick succeeded where Peter continually failed. He made her feel wanted and chased. For the last nine months, her physical activities with Patrick extended way beyond the gym floor. She pretended to struggle on the last rep just to feel his hands tighten around her arms and assist her in getting the weight bar back on the rack. She looked up at him from the bench press, her chest rising and falling from both the exercise and the stirring of her heart by his words of wanting.

"Don't make it hard for me, Pat, let's finish this workout and then I'll make your wait worthwhile," she said.

Patrick looked down and could not help but notice her nipples rising and pushing through her leotard. "You are an exquisitely, beautiful woman. Looks to me like you might already have other things on your mind," he said.

"Stop! You know what you do to me when you talk like that," protested Claire.

Together, Patrick and Claire sweated it out for the next hour. Then, as per their usual routine, Claire showered at the gym while Patrick went back to his place. Twenty-five minutes later, he was closing the front door behind Claire, taking her in his arms and tightly squeezing her body close to his as they passionately kissed. Stumbling towards the bedroom, he had her shirt unbuttoned before they collapsed together on his bed.

"Two hours?" Patrick whispered into her ear, "it's never long enough…"

"I know, I know, but that's the way it is for now. You know that. Let's make the afternoon count while we have it," said Claire, rolling on top of Patrick and fumbling with his belt buckle.

It was nearly three-thirty before she got home and starting making her notes for her call with Hedgestone. She checked her email and interestingly, found an incoming mail from Jane.

Hi Claire,

Please find attached a draft response to the landlord. I can't see any major issues with the lease renewal, so long as you respond to their requests for the certificate of currency for insurances, as well as a copy of the maintenance contract for the air conditioning and other property services. I will leave it to you. Hope it goes well, let me know if you need any further assistance.

Best regards,
Jane Johnson.

'Hmm, all relatively tame,' thought Claire. She quickly found Hedgestone's Skype ID and clicked the green phone icon. Hedgestone picked up immediately.

"Hedgestone," he answered gruffly.

"Oh, hi, Pastor Hedgestone, it's Claire."

"Claire Endor, the redeemed witch of Whitehaven. Are you well?"

"Yes, fighting fit, thank you, and you? I imagine you are in full swing for your international global bible conference next month?" said Claire.

"We most certainly are. I've just booked the biggest auditorium we have ever used. We are expecting between nine and ten thousand people," said Hedgestone, with more than an ounce of pride and bravado. Numbers, noise and nickels were his constant KPI companions.

"Very exciting, Pastor. Wish we could be there. Anyway, you asked me to give you an update on Jane Johnson. So, I managed to have a coffee with her under the guise of assisting our admin property team with a lease renewal and review of increases and..."

"Wait a minute, wait a minute," interrupted Hedgestone. "Are you saying you have involved her in our internal business affairs?"

"Well, I needed to create a connection point and as she is a lawyer, I gave her a copy of the church property lease and asked her to respond to the landlord to exercise our renewal option just as per instruction from the last business management meeting, so that..."

Again, Hedgestone cut Claire off.

"You what?! Just how stupid of a witch bitch are you? The last thing we want is to have this trollop crawling all over our internal affairs. The mission was to find out what she was up to in Africa — not invite her into our confidential business. You better fix this! I thought you said you knew how to deal with a white rabbit? Why is she still breathing?! Women like you are good for nothing more than a hole in the fence. Don't call me again unless you have some real news or you will be looking for a new job!"

Hedgestone cut the call before Claire could respond.

Claire was shaking, her hands fumbling to try and get the headphones off. Finally, she threw them at the screen and stared blankly at it, while biting her thumbnails and shaking her head.

The thought of losing her position in the ministry was terrifying. She knew how Hedgestone removed people and had watched him at work many times. And her philandering husband, Peter, had given him plenty to work with.

She thought about Patrick and wondered if Hedgestone knew about him. Fear drilled down deeper into her soul and began tightening its grip. It played out the whole scene in her head. Hedgestone would announce that she and Peter would step down from their ministry for 'redirection.' Then he would silently but strategically release through his channels that their marriage was a charade and had fallen into infidelity. He would go on to have meetings with her peers to encourage them to join his concern and prayer for the restoration of the Endor's but secretly would have them disgraced and stripped of all involvement in leadership for years until they realised they had no future with GoF.

Claire held her head in her hands. "That smart arse bitch, Jane — I have to get rid of her," she told herself.

An equally present and opposite thought also entered her head, and she wondered why she had been too afraid to think of it before. Just why was Hedgestone so inflamed by this Jane? What was it that she had supposed to have done? But then she disciplined herself that she obviously didn't need to know or Hedgestone would have told her. She had a chance to be useful to Hedgestone and would focus on that now more than ever. This time she would not let him down…

CHAPTER 25

SIBLINGS REUNITED

Tommy and Jane both knew that if they were to execute on their plan effectively, they had a lot of work to do. That night at dinner, Tommy laid out his strategy to bring Hedgestone to justice. He called it Project Monument. All of his research and investigations indicated that Hedgestone had indeed once been part of a unique and genuine spirit-filled movement. A movement that impacted thousands of lives across many nations and people groups. A movement that enlisted many other workers and contributors − people like Jane's parents. But over the years, that passionate movement had become a stone cold, dead monument, overtaken by greed and self-preservation, which became prioritised above the needs of others − the very purpose on which it had been founded.

It was empty of anything warm and alive. All that remained were the dead man's bones of religious rules and regulations, controlling fear and intimidation. Tommy had taken up the challenge to be the forensic coroner that would deliver the results of his post mortem examination on that dead carcass to anybody who would listen. And in the process, he had inadvertently set up a monumental Lot's Wife pillar point of reference for everyone else − this is what happens when you do the sort of stuff that Hedgestone does.

Jane had listened intently to Tommy's plan and challenged it where she thought it was weak or lacked the necessary detail. Together they collaborated and consecrated themselves to its fulfilment. They prepared hundreds of pages of supporting documentation, fully referenced and indexed, ready for a rapid discovery after their planned 'big bang' moment.

The GOF's annual conference event provided the pinnacle focus point of their strategy. Conveniently, Hedgestone was gathering everyone into one place at one time. There was no better opportunity for Jane and Tommy to execute. This gave them three months to prepare. It was clear to them that they needed someone based in the US on the inside of GOF if they were to succeed in their ambitions. They both thought that Paul might be the one that could fill this position. It seemed fitting for them to reconnect and for Paul to be a part of the efforts to bring about some justice for his parents. In any event, Jane had felt it was not right that she did not share with him what they had discovered these last few weeks.

They had decided that Jane should contact Paul, introduce Tommy and lay out their thoughts before him. It was Friday night, and Jane had left her commercial concerns at the office for the week. She had emailed Paul a few days before to set up a Skype video chat for tonight. Jane had tried to work through in her mind just how to present some of this difficult family history but in the end, decided she did not want a planned conversation. She wanted the call to be as natural and flowing as it could be, as it had been nearly a year since they last spoke. She guessed that that was because, in many ways, their communication reminded each other of their complicated and somewhat painful pasts. Trauma always sought to find a way to replay itself in their lives, like a broken record, an unresolved circular reference. Jane had always wanted to break out of that uncomfortable zone, and wondered if this might just be the catalyst they needed to facilitate this. After all, although they were orphans, they were still family — the only family each of them had.

Without further hesitation, Jane clicked on Paul's Skype icon, which happened to be a nice-looking cello.

"Hello, Jane!" came Paul's voice over the connection, loud and clear.

"Hey Paul, so good to hear your voice. Are you OK if we enable video?" said Jane.

"Sure, how's that? I can see you fine — seems a good connection. You are looking well. Thanks for organising the chat. It's so easy for time to pass without catching up. So, what have you been up to, Sis?"

"Well, I have to tell you, I've been back to Africa, and a lot of things have happened that have really changed me. For a start, you and I need to see a lot more of each other, Paul. I know you've got your music school pursuits in the States, but we are all the family we have left, and we can't let that slip away, year by year. You're my brother. We went through a great deal together, and we survived." Jane found herself jumping into the heart of the matter without any courtesy small talk.

"Africa! Really?" said Paul. "That's a courageous move, Jane. And yes, although I've been relationally lazy, you have to know you are frequently in my thoughts. You won't believe this, but I often want to reach out for my big sis and talk things through with you because you were always there for me. But something always overcomes and restrains me. You know I buried myself in my music because at the time, it was the only thing that gave me any relief from the disconnection and absence of belonging that I felt after we lost Mum and Dad. I was able to create my own space and place and begin to define and shape all of those emotions and crucible events with my own interpretations of other works from lots of great musicians. And guess what? It really gave my own work its authenticity. I haven't told you this, but I might even get something published soon, and, more news for you, I might get the opportunity to relocate back to Sydney and take up a position with the Sydney Symphonic Orchestra. I've got some auditions coming up in a few months. So, Africa, what was that all about then? What made you want to do that?"

Jane was incredibly excited at Paul's unexpected news that he might be coming home. She was also both relieved and buoyed up by the openness and easiness of the conversation. She was concerned it might be awkward in some way, but not at all.

"With the SSO? Amazing Paul. Keep me posted if there is anything I can do for you from this end. You know that you are more than welcome to stay at my place if you ever need to. OK, Africa – a long story and something I did want to talk through with you. Do you have time now?" asked Jane.

"I am all ears and eyes," confirmed Paul.

"Well, do you remember Sipho Mbane, Dad's ministry assistant in Maputo?

"Yeah, I do actually. Nice guy. Dad relied on him a lot from what I recall."

"He wrote me a letter a few weeks back. Completely out of the blue, unexpected, as I've not spoken to him for years since we left. Following that, we had a long phone chat. He told me some very disturbing things about the passing of our parents and who might have been involved. He asked if I could come to Africa, and everything would be explained," Jane paused.

"Go on," said Paul, listening more intently now.

Over the next hour, Jane poured out her heart to her brother about that terrible time in their lives thirteen years ago and who they had learned was responsible. They cried together through much of it, especially as Jane shared the visit to their parents' graves. They each confessed their long-held feelings of remorse that they had not tried harder to care for each other. Jane expressed her sheer helplessness as she watched a tender-hearted young boy who so loved and admired his father, torn away from him without warning, stripped of all that he desperately needed, just when that boy was becoming a man.

Paul talked of the anger that had burned hot within him like a furious volcano; of the consuming fury he held towards a faceless foe – a thief of life and purpose. Of how that fury came to be directed towards any face that reached out to him, including Jane. It wasn't long before Paul was filled with the same ambitions as Jane in working together to bring Hedgestone to justice, although he was not entirely sure how he could help. Jane went on to share how Tommy Cacao had become more than a friend through these events, of how she had come to rely on him emotionally and wanted to be with him more and more. Before they knew it, the clock began to intrude on their continuing discussion.

"Hey Jane, I'm going to need to leave for rehearsals soon. It's already seven-thirty am here. I am both grieved but glad for the chance to talk all this through. We need to talk again soon. Anyway, like I said, I might be in Sydney in a month and would love to meet your Mr Cacao. I do vaguely remember him. It is quite a lot to work through and digest. Give me some time, but yes if I can help your plans in any way, of course, I'll do it."

"No problem, Paul. Yes, we'll talk again soon. So exciting that you might be coming down our way. Bye now, love you." Jane clicked and closed the skype session. A feeling of great relief came over Jane as she felt her burden being lightened significantly by sharing it with Paul. That she might be seeing him soon was also stirring some high expectation in her heart.

Paul, on the other hand, although he was equally glad to catch up with his sister, felt as if the past he had longed to leave behind over many years was now beginning to creep back up on him. But he knew within himself that this time, he had the chance for it to be finally confronted and resolved. How he had missed his dad as a young teenage boy when he felt he needed him most! And the suddenness of it all had left him distraught and disconnected for a long time.

That morning, he went found himself going through the motions of prep for rehearsal with the string group he had been working with, but struggled to concentrate. The news from Jane was distracting him more than he had anticipated. His focus had somehow moved away from the pursuit of professional musical perfection. There was something new in his heart that now took priority and precedence. The notes fell off the manuscript page, and in their place, his parents' faces emerged. Feelings he thought he had buried long ago now began to resurface. Times with his father, setting up equipment in the church together or watching a Mozambique sunset with an ice cream from the elevated back porch of their home. And then the ghost of his mother — he could still feel her soft hands on his face, and looking back into hers, smiling and comforting. He knew that nothing he could do would bring back those times. However, the compelling urge to validate his parent's lives and bring retrospective correction to their untimely passing was fast becoming overwhelming.

CHAPTER 26

DEPTHS OF DARKNESS

When you do something wrong — something violently wrong that goes against one's own conscience, one's own internal governance — and then bury it deep and think no one has noticed or will ever find out, you create a life overhead — an increasingly heavy burden upon heart and mind, a debt of possible discovery that becomes a living presence and inhabits your daily thought-life with no escape.

Reasoning and wrestling with arguments of self-justification for your actions may appear to provide temporary relief, but it's a deception. The violation just finds another way to eat up more of life's 'in the moment' presence and enjoyment. The cycle ends with increased condemnation as yet another argument is explored, only to be found wanting and weighed without substantiation for a cause. You become randomly distant in conversations with others. You descend into a blurry, unfocused view of any task set before you. Years and decades can pass until time has eaten up your soul from the inside out, leaving you nothing more than a weak and helpless empty shell with no more soul purpose than a cockroach.

Hedgestone knew this better than most. After all, he was a preacher and a good one. His grasp of the Word of God in analysis, analogy and application was brilliant. His commitment to studying, with hours and hours spent in absorbing commentaries and lexicons and etymological word meanings, was by far more dedicated than any of his peers. But it was also merciless, delivered without grace, love or forgiveness. Conviction and weeping condemnation — yes, that was his specialty. Getting people onto their knees at the altar, with a wailing and gnashing of teeth – that was his goal. Create an environment of self-despising and unworthiness so that they were dependent upon him for any sense of personal value. Restoration, redemption and recovery were not considered essential deliverables from his pulpit. Get them to feel guilt, bind them in chains of low self-worth and you could have people follow you anywhere, give more than they ever expected and do whatever you asked them to do. Hedgestone had perfected this craft over many years. To the 'saved' in his church, he would say, "You owe me your soul." Ownership was his goal when he peered out upon his congregation every Sunday from those steely squinted blue eyes. Always the proprietor in thought and word, and never the pilgrim in venture or deed.

David sending Uriah to the war and placing him on the front lines, in the heat of battle, to face certain death, just so he could take his wife, Bathsheba. Yes, he preached it, and with great eloquence. But not to the conviction of his own conscience – only his battered and beaten flock. Saul's estranged sanity and indulgent backslidings with the occult and his witch of Endor because of the madness in his pursuit of David, Hedgestone had explored every psychotic episode and projected the scenarios onto his congregation. They were like lambs to the slaughter in his hands. Cain's murder of his brother Abel in hatred of his brother's acceptance before the Lord, his consequential rejection and expulsion to the land of Nod in broken fellowship, as his brother's blood cried out to the Lord – this was the material that Hedgestone loved to explore. Yes, it was the word of God, but only the brave would challenge him if it represented the whole counsel of God or the needs of his humble congregation that were mostly consumed with the daily grind of paying the bills and keeping their jobs.

His analysis was so in-depth and told with such riveting evidentiary relevance because, in most cases, it was nothing more than a personal inquisition of his own thought life and behaviour over a period of 40 years. But dissecting and condemning every failure of the human condition did nothing to heal his own. Accusation and observation without personal repentance only increased the burden of judgement he increasingly felt, from which there was no escape.

Still, year after year, Hedgestone ploughed on. But never a word on the woman caught in adultery and the sending away of her accusers as there was no one without sin that could pitch a stone. Nothing about the longing of a loving father for a prodigal son, the peering down the road with longing every morning and every evening for a possible return. And not one mention of the look of love from a bloodied and beaten Jesus across a courtyard to his friend and disciple, Peter, even as Peter swore and denied he ever knew him. No interest in these texts from Hedgestone.

Hedgestone was not comfortable with love or forgiveness or mercy. He felt everyone's life should be as difficult as his own had been. The ministry was a business to be done. Just execute the motions without emotion, affection or kindness — both were a weakness to him. His task was to raise strong soldiers that would fight for their earthly general — not build a family or connect lives with a saviour. Did the Spirit of God inhabit his sermons, or something far more sinister? A counterfeit spirit, carnal and manipulative of the will of man's hearts, empowered by the self-indulgent authority of the platform and not the comfort of the Holy Spirit? He had successfully sensualised the spirit of God, rather than spiritualise the senses of his hearers. They could not hear what God had to say because Hedgestone's pitch was deafening. They could not see what God had before them because Hedgestone was constantly in the way. They could not feel the comfort of the Holy Spirit because Hedgestone so scorched and bruised them that the only thing they felt was continual unworthiness.

This is why the Johnsons incident so plagued him. Although there were many violations of his ministry, obligations and contradictions to his life testimony, this was undoubtedly a big-ticket item. This was the one that he wanted to erase but never could. He thought he was done with it, so many years ago. But now it reared its head again. Like Abel's spilt blood crying out from the ground for judgement, so too Dale and Dominique Johnson could reach from beyond the grave in a far away, obscure dusty African cemetery and demand vindication. Sacrificed in the battle for the personal gratification of a lustful general, no different to Uriah the Hittite, the only difference between David the King and Hedgestone was that David repented when Nathan pointed the bony finger. But who could cry out, 'Thou art the man' to Hedgestone? Indeed, no one from within, as Hedgestone had made himself accountable to no one, either internally or externally among peers. That's why he feared Jane like he had feared no one ever before.

Chapter 27

A Winter Warmer

Jane could not stop thinking about her conversation with Paul. That Skype chat was probably one of the best talks they had had since they were kids, before their parents had died. All this time, there had been this invisible elephant-size obstruction between them. They had both become so cocooned in the embalmed lives they had made for themselves that they could never really reach out and touch each other. Politeness and superficialities kept things cordial and impersonal. Even though they had both wanted something more — something more precious and more profound in connection as brother and sister — there seemed to be something pushing them apart whenever they tried to draw close, almost like the repulsive energy of like-signed magnets, they had never seemed to be able to connect with words or touch each other's hearts.

Tonight, that had changed, thought Jane as she disconnected from the Skype session. She felt a thrill and excitement as though she had found something that had been lost for so long. Jane now knew without a doubt that Paul cared about the same things she did. That together, they could experience a long-awaited redemption and finally answer all of the why's that had plagued them over the last 13 years. Rather than live separate lives because it seemed less painful than the reminder of the life that was, now they could not wait to get together and bring about accountability. The prospect did not intimidate them one iota — they had nothing to lose. The way out of their emotional isolation was simple: bring Hedgestone to justice and judgement by his own, and in doing so, maybe set free a generation of faithful believers caught in his deception.

It was time to catch up with Tommy. So much to share about Paul. It was time to get on with the plan. Besides all of that, she just wanted to be with him again. 'Text or phone call?' she thought to herself. A text would be a casual prompt, perhaps? A phone call too direct maybe? Well, it was out of work hours, she thought and not too late, and so he should be able to take a call, Jane reasoned as she found him in her favourites folder and pressed his smiling face.

"Hi, Jane," came Tommy's bright voice after only two rings. "What's going on?"

"Tommy, are you well?"

"Yes, all good here."

"What are you up to?" pried and prodded Jane, wanting a little bit more life detail to be shared beyond an 'all good here.'

"Oh, you know, just pondering the many and varied vagaries of life. Just got back from the gym, took a shower and was feeling too lazy to cook. Thought I might just reach for the two-minute noodles or a Vegemite and cheese toastie. My Portuguese mother and amazing cook would turn in her grave if she heard me say that, but such is the life of a financially oppressed pro bono, bachelor lawyer."

"Do I hear the strains of self-pity as only the male pathos can express?" stirred Jane. "Why don't I pick you up in 15 mins for something healthier like some steamed dumplings and jasmine tea?"

Tommy turned the thought over in his mind for less than a split second. "You know what, that sounds like exactly what I need! How do you do this?"

"Do what?" asked Jane.

"Sense the moment and know exactly what I need."

"Well, call it female intuition if you like. Anyway, I just had the most amazing call with Paul. I need to share it with you," Jane confessed, with a hint of longing.

"Get your skates on, I'll be waiting outside in 10 minutes."

It was 12 minutes before Jane spotted Tommy in a hoody and jeans standing at the curb outside his apartment block, anxiously peering up the road in the opposite direction of her approach. Time for some fun, she thought as she slowed to a crawl just behind him and tooted her horn with a touch of aggression that had the desired effect in startling him.

"A well-timed text would have been more than adequate," complained Tommy as he jumped back into his skin and got into Jane's car.

"Oh, poor Tommy. There's no fun or spontaneity in a well-timed text," returned Jane.

Tommy knew by now not to take Jane on in such a tit-for-tat battle, as she was far ahead of him when it came to jibes and jostling. "So, Jane, where are we off too?" he asked.

"Well, this new place opened up not too far from you. I've meant to try it for a while — Shanghai Dumplings."

Ten minutes later, Jane and Tommy were warming up with a jasmine tea and selection of steamed pastry delicacies. Jane poured her heart out to Tommy about the relief she felt to finally connect again with Paul in a meaningful way. Tommy again proved himself a great and patient listener, silently nodding and allowing Jane to empty herself of her words and emotions, his dark eyes full of empathy and comfort. He used the silence to admire and soak up every facial expression and nuance in Jane's voice. When he felt she had finished her story, he thought it might be appropriate to intervene before she could start another one and, without words, silently pushed the bamboo steamer basket with one remaining dumpling in Jane's direction.

He succeeded in breaking Jane's train of thought as she looked down and seriously considered the dumpling distraction.

"Thanks, are you sure you don't want it?" she asked, already with chopsticks in hand.

"Go ahead," said Tommy and then quickly moved into the conversation space he had created. "I don't think we need to worry about getting Paul out to Australia. We can use him in the US to fulfil the sound engineer role in our plan. We just need to get on a Skype call and walk him through his part. Remember, the goal is to make Hedgestone accountable and judged by his own."

Jane nodded in agreement. "OK, I get it. But I would so like to see him."

"Yeah, but what if Hedgestone's people see him here? At the moment, he is the wildcard operative. They know you. They have seen me. Did I tell you I think I was followed home from your house the other night?" said Tommy. "And remember, there is only two months to the big annual conference. You need to start working on your part. You are going to have to haul in extreme emotions and be the fast and quick-minded, thinking-on-your-feet, interviewer that I know you can be. If you want to pull this off, we have a lot of work to do."

Jane looked at Tommy and realised that he was serious and appreciated the reality check.

"You're right, you're right. Let's go through the plan with Paul on the weekend. But its Friday night. Let's unwind for now. Come back to my place for a nightcap and some ice cream."

Tommy settled the dinner bill, and together they entered a grey and cold winter's night. Whether it was the one glass of red wine at dinner or the icy July wind blowing into her, Jane was seeking warmth of all kinds and seamlessly slipped her arm inside Tommy's and pressed in close to him with her head to his shoulder. Tommy received the gesture without response and took her hand in his as they found their way to the car. Jane surrendered her hand to the strength of his and felt again that same growing and glowing feeling of safety, security and peacefulness when she was with Tommy. Trust and respect had grown between them, two qualities that Jane highly valued. He had become her sanctuary and place of refuge from an emotionally painful personal past and the fierce commercial, often lonely, present of law practice. They separated quickly and made a dash for each side of the car as rain started to fall. They slammed the car doors behind them, trying to keep the cold out.

"Are our winters getting colder or am I just getting…?" Tommy was about to say "older," but Jane had decided she had another way to deal with the weather. She reached across from the drivers' side of the car and with both hands sliding through Tommy's thick black hair, pulled his head towards her and found his lips with hers, reaching in with all the fullness of desire that had built up for some time. Although absolutely taken by surprise, Tommy yielded to the moment her lips were on his. He responded immediately and reached out his arms to embrace Jane amidst all of the awkwardness of the cramped space. Pressed towards her, feeling the softness of her face against his, he found himself regretting for a moment that he had not shaved.

They mutually pulled away for a moment. Jane's desire-filled eyes looked into Tommy's dark pools as she quietly whispered, "Do you feel any warmer now? I've been waiting and wanting to do that for the longest time."

Tommy stared back into Jane's and gently reached in to softly kiss her again with a confirming response that left Jane in no doubt that he had fully welcomed her initiatives. His large and spread-out hands moved down behind her neck to her back, gently pressing and pulling her into him.

"Warm and fuzzy all over," Tommy answered. "But if we stay here like this much longer, I am going to have a total meltdown."

"You're right. Come on, let's get home. I've got some hot chocolate and fresh strawberries waiting for you," said Jane.

Jane gathered herself back into the driver's seat and fumbled for the keys. There was no doubt Jane drove a little faster than usual, the distraction of Tommy's outreached arm and hand caressing the back of her neck not helping with her concentration at all. Nonetheless, she leant back into his hand and enjoyed the moment for all it was worth. It wasn't long before she was parking in the apartment basement and waiting for the elevator, politely nodding to a young family that lived on the floor above hers. The elevator doors opened, and Tommy was about to follow the family in front of him when he felt Jane tug on his sleeve.

"Let's take the next one over here," said Jane, leading Tommy to the second lift doors just opening. As soon as the doors closed, again they found themselves in each other's arms for all of the twenty-three seconds it took to get to the seventh floor. Jane and Tommy stumbled into Jane's apartment with expectancy and passion pounding in their hearts. Tonight they would suspend all of their schemes and plans for some self-indulgence of another kind. So much so, that Jane did not notice that the bedside lamp was switched on in her bedroom, when in fact, it had been off since she had left home that morning.

CHAPTER 28

A WITCH IN WAITING

Claire Endor was possession-driven to offer up to Hedgestone his white rabbit. She knew she could do it. She knew it was critical to Hedgestone even if she didn't know why. "True love," he had told her, "is a sacrifice," and she was determined to bring him hers. Mentally, she had prepared herself for the task.

The week before, she had made a decision — it was time for Patrick, the gym stud, to go. She could not afford any loose ends. After their last assignation, like a black widow spider, she had confronted her prey. "You want life to be an endless euphoric orgasm when, in fact, there are some things in life that don't last beyond the moment — and you Pat are just that. Just for the moment. Goodbye, and thanks for the workout!"

She had waited and watched Jane's movements for many days. How she despised her beauty, intelligent innocence, and what she interpreted as an I'm-better-than-you attitude. It was time, she thought, to get this done. Earlier that evening, she had watched from her car as Jane drove off into the night to pick up Tommy for their Asian night out. Now was her chance.

Using Jane's security pass, taken from her bag at the café that day, Claire discreetly found her way into Jane's apartment. She made a short tour around Jane's home. In the kitchen, she selected herself a sharp but short, six-inch carving knife from the bench set. Then to the ensuite bathroom where she ran a bath. Her plan was simple. This was to look like the suicide of a successful but lonely lawyer. Back to the bedroom, she waited by the window overlooking the street entrance to the underground carpark. Finally, two hours later, she heard the front door open. But what Claire wasn't expecting, was the sound of Tommy's voice behind Jane. Her heart rate quickened, as did her mind, as it came up with a new plan of how she could take care of both of them.

"Strawberries and hot chocolate I think was the promise," Tommy reminded Jane, as he closed the door quietly behind him.

Claire panicked. Her heart jumped, and she felt the adrenalin race through her from head to toe. She knew her limitations. It would be challenging to take on two of them. Claire was confident she could easily overpower and take out Jane, but not the well-built Tommy as well. There was no way out as she crouched behind the door of the bathroom. Thoughts of failure and Hedgestone's damming voice raced through her heart.

"Yes, but you have to help," Jane answered Tommy. "I will do the hot chocolate, but you see if you can cut up those cold strawberries in the fridge and sprinkle a little icing sugar on top."

'These two make me sick,' thought Claire to herself. 'I would love to stick it them both.'

Tommy opened the fridge, found the strawberries and went to work on slicing and dicing. Jane was busy frothing milk and chocolate and didn't notice Tommy coming up behind her. With a rosy red strawberry in his mouth, he grabbed her from behind and turned her around. Gently he found her lips and pushed the strawberry into Jane's mouth. Jane playfully received it and together, they extracted every ounce of juice between them. When the fruit was all but gone, they continued to explore each other's mouths while Tommy drew her in close.

"You have a very inquisitive tongue," remarked Jane as she drew back for breath.

"You don't know just how inquisitive it can be. Perhaps you want to find out?" challenged Tommy before resuming his attentions on Jane.

Jane flushed with excitement at the thought of what Tommy might have in mind but managed to reign in her passion for a moment.

"Let's not let the hot chocolate lose its temperature. Come, let's sit down," said Jane as she disentangled herself and led the way with the mugs to the lounge, Tommy following behind with the bowl of icing covered strawberries.

Jane settled into the corner of the couch, pulling up and crossing her legs, so she could face Tommy at the other end. She playfully sipped on her hot chocolate.

"Now that will warm you up on the inside, Mr Cacao," she said.

"I'm already warmed up on the inside," said Tommy, "but yes, it's a nice winter warmer. I could not think of anywhere else I would like to be." Tommy drank deeply without taking his eyes off Jane.

Tommy's words were stirring things in Jane far more than his strawberry kisses. She held his gaze and absorbed the moment, warmed by the steaming beverage in her hand.

"Tommy, I'm going to be as honest as I have ever been with anyone in my life. I have come to love you with all that is in me. When this is all over, I want to be with you. All the time. Every day." Her pooling, large as ever baby blue eyes echoed her words, piercing straight into Tommy's soul.

That's it. She had said it. She had wanted to say that for the longest time, and now it was done. It was out there and wasn't coming back.

Tommy put his mug down on the table and reached in close to Jane. He gently cupped her face with both hands and looked straight back into those soul windows. "I promise you, Jane, when this is over, when we have fully vindicated your parents, I'm going to look after you with all that I am."

Tommy sealed his words and his promise with the softest of kisses. His hands began to slide down over Jane's shoulders to her lower back, and he pulled her close to him, feeling her breast rise and fall against his chest as she returned his embrace. Then after a moment of enjoying this mutual indulgence, he whispered in Jane's ear, "But until then let's take this slowly and not spoil anything."

Jane could not help but praise his wisdom and self-control. "You're right," she said, with a fraction of disappointment, a bit like a kid on Christmas Eve wanting to unwrap her presents then and there. "You had better finish your chocolate, and I will seal wrap those strawberries for you to take home," she said with a fragile discipline.

Tommy reigned in his passions and withdrew to his corner of the couch. Ever so slowly, he took up his mug and savoured every mouthful of the warm beverage. Minutes passed as they continued to drink in each other's presence. Finally, Tommy picked up his phone.

"I'm gonna book me an Uber," he quietly announced.

'Finally!' thought Claire as she turned over the blade between her fingers. Tommy's self-control would be her opportunity to end this nauseating little romance. Even better, when it was all done, Tommy might even blame himself for leaving Jane that night.

"OK, well, thank you for a delightful evening. I'll call you tomorrow?" prompted Jane.

"Sure," replied Tommy, standing up to go, grabbing his jacket and glancing at his phone. "Looks like I've got some drivers close by."

Jane stood to meet him and helped him rug up for the ride home. She put her arms around him for a last goodbye kiss as she walked him to the door. Tommy opened the front door and turned before walking out, "Sleep tight, see you tomorrow," he grinned cheekily at Jane and quietly closed the door behind him.

Jane lent back against the door as it closed, content and satisfied that she could let her feelings be known by Tommy and that he fully reciprocated them with his own. She collected the mugs on the table and noticed that Tommy had forgot his strawberries on the coffee table. She thought to herself that perhaps she should have asked him to stay but knew that time would come if she were patient.

She made her way to the bathroom, completely lost in her own thoughts and failed to notice that a bath had been drawn. She stood before the vanity mirror and looked deep into her reflection. How long since she had felt such a sense of settled happiness and expectation? Could she actually be this close to finding a love that would fill that guarded void of singleness?

Just then, Claire slowly closed the bathroom door she had been crouching behind.

With an overwhelming shock, Jane saw the door close behind her in the mirror and Claire slowly rise over her shoulder.

"Claire! What on earth are you doing here?" Jane inquired, confusion and fear rattling her voice.

"I've been waiting, oh so patiently for you, dear Jane. I thought that the soppy strawberry lover boy would never leave and I would have to deal with both of you."

"What are you talking about Claire? You shouldn't be here."

"Well Jane, you have been causing a great deal of trouble, haven't you? Pastor Hedgestone is extremely concerned about your activities. He tells me you have been stirring up things that should have been left well alone and we can't have you doing that. You know the bible says to *mark them that cause division among you…have nothing to do with them…give them over to Satan*, and that's precisely what we need to take care of tonight." Claire finished by raising the knife in her hand for Jane to see, enjoying the terror in her eyes.

"Wait, Claire, you don't know what Hedgestone has been up to all these years," said Jane as she backed away from the slowly approaching Claire. How she now wished she had asked Tommy to stay!

Meanwhile, Tommy was just making his way past the apartment concierge, feeling quite warm and fuzzy on the inside when he realised, 'The strawberries! I forgot to take the strawberries!' Now he found himself facing a dilemma. He looked at his phone. The Uber was still five mins away. He had time to go back upstairs and collect them. But how would Jane interpret that? That he had changed his mind and wanted to stay the night? Maybe he should just go home? Perhaps he should text her?

'No,' he thought, 'I'm going to go back and get them. Jane might think I did not appreciate the thought of the gift.' He made his way back to the elevator and waited for the lift.

Seven floors above, Claire was closing in on Jane. "Time for you to take a bath, cutie. After all that steamy romance, you must be all hot and sweaty."

Jane backed away from the blade Claire flashed in front of her, towards the towel rail behind her.

"Claire, you are making a mistake. Hedgestone isn't worth it. He is creaming the church finances. And he arranged the hi-jacking of my parents fourteen years ago," Jane pleaded.

Claire was momentarily taken aback by Jane's allegations, but very quickly, her devotion to Hedgestone grew even stronger. "He's more like me then I thought," she took note.

Finally, Tommy's lift arrived, and he made his way up to level 7.

Inside her apartment bathroom, Jane could see the hatred in Claire's eyes and knew she needed to do something quickly. She reached behind her and grabbed the towel on the rail. In an instant, she had wrapped it around the knife in Claire's hand, and pulled her behind her. Claire was not expecting any resistance and was taken by surprise as she fell to the floor but quickly reached out to grab Jane's ankle. Jane kicked behind her and managed to open the bathroom door and make a run for the front door, screaming for help as she went. Claire picked herself up and ran after her.

Tommy had just got out of the elevator and thought he heard Jane cry for help. He bolted for her door and called out to her.

"Jane! What's going on?" yelled Tommy as he wrestled with the locked door.

Finally, Jane made it to the front door and opened it.

"Tommy! It's Claire — she's got a knife!" cried Jane.

Just then, Claire appeared in the lounge, still brandishing the knife menacingly towards them both. Claire knew she had lost her chance and now needed to make a run for it.

"Get out of my way, or one of you is going down," she threatened.

Tommy stepped in front of Jane and slowly made towards Claire. "Claire, you don't need to do this. Think about it. Hedgestone is not worth it. Look what he has turned you into," Tommy attempted to reason.

"Back away from the door!" demanded Claire. "You have no idea what I'm capable of," she threatened.

"OK, OK," said Tommy, stepping inside the apartment, Jane close behind, and leaving the front door open.

Claire made her way to the door as she sneered "Don't think this is over!" and with that, turned and made a run for it.

Tommy quickly closed and latched the door behind her. Turning to Jane, he grabbed her, asking, "Are you OK! Are you OK?"

"Yes, yes," said Jane. "I'm fine. Thank God you were still here."

"Well, I came back for my strawberries. You forgot to give them to me. Quite thoughtless of you actually," Tommy jibed, trying to de-escalate what had just happened.

"I can't believe it. Claire was waiting for me all night in the bathroom! Did you see the look in her eyes? Hedgestone knows we are up to something, and somehow he has activated Claire to come after me. This is a whole lot more serious than what I thought."

Jane dropped down on the couch with her face in her hands. Tommy sat down beside her with an arm around her shoulders and tried to offer some comfort.

Jane turned towards him, "We can't go to the police — it would undo everything we've planned".

Tommy looked at Jane with a serious face, "Thank God you are OK."

Jane flung her arms around Tommy and buried her face in the well of his neck. He felt her warm tears on his skin as he heard the faint whimpers and sniffles of her crying.

"Please stay," she asked Tommy.

"Hey, it's OK, I'm here now. No one is going to hurt you tonight," Tommy whispered in her ear as his large hands moved through her hair and held her head in his hands. He felt Jane's clinging arms holding him tight and her chest against his, rising and falling with still anxious breaths. One hand slipped softly across his cheek as she turned his face towards hers. This time, she planted a knowing and passionate kiss on Tommy's mouth. As Tommy received her embrace and returned her affectionate kisses with his own, Jane pulled him down on top of her as she dropped back on to the couch. Her hands were sliding up underneath his shirt, and the touch of his skin in her hands began to send rushes of expectation and excitement through her body.

"I've wanted to feel you next to me for so long," Tommy heard her whisper as he fumbled with the buttons of her blouse with one hand, her heaving chest beneath him; his other hand slipping up beneath her skirt and firmly squeezing her thigh. His touch sent passion pulsating through her groin and midriff, which she lifted and ground into Tommy.

Whether it was the shock of the confrontation with Claire or the heat of the moment, finally Jane surrendered to her deep and longing desires.

"Let's go to bed," she whispered in Tommy's ear.

They untangled themselves and rose together, Jane leading Tommy by the hand, leaving behind a perfectly prepared if lonely-looking bowl of icing sugar-coated strawberries on the coffee table.

CHAPTER 29

THE END OF ENDOR

Claire cursed all the way back to her car as she sped off into the night.

A thousand thoughts raced through her head. How could she fail Hedgestone like this? Why didn't she finish off Jane when she had the chance? What did Jane mean about skimming the church finances and having her parents hijacked? What happens now? What if they go to the police? What will Hedgestone do to her?

She had no evidence that she was acting under instruction from Hedgestone. What should she do now? Run? Hide? Finally, she reached a conclusion. There was actually only one response that was in her control. By the time she got home, she had made up her mind.

With her heart filled with darkness, isolation and bitterness, Claire ran her own bath, stripped down and stepped into the warm water. She picked up her shaving razor and took out the blade and slowly ran her thumb down the blade, not flinching as it drew blood. Claire looked closely at her wrist and found a nice plump vein. Slowly she sliced into it, downwards not across, to maximise the incision. She marvelled as the claret red blood began to spurt out of her body and dropped her arm into the water as she leant back into its warmth to overcome the coldness that began to overtake her body as the warm blood and life drained out of her.

The futility of her past began to emerge from a sea of dark places in front of her. Like shadowy faceless figures, they began to draw closer and surround her. The salvation that she thought she had received, which for a time, had filled her hope, seemed to shrink away in the distance as if she was sliding down a slippery slope in slow motion. At the same time, she confronted the fullness of her error in leaving behind her personal relationship with Jesus for obedience to a man with a covetous cause wrapped up in the presence of false religion – it all replayed itself before her with an ever-increasing, screaming crescendo of despair. Minutes later, a mocking, laughing darkness, appeared and stood over her, filling her with terror. Her eyes closed as Claire slipped below the waters of the bath and into eternity, breathing her last breath.

The news of Claire's death shocked her ministry team and employers at GOF church. Hedgestone dealt with it masterfully and to his full advantage. His people had known full well about her liaisons with Pat, the personal trainer, as well as her husband, Peter's, philandering.

"This is what happens when you lead a double life, a life of lust and carnal indulgence, of unrepentance and stubborn self-will and manipulation," Hedgestone told the Australian church leadership in his debriefing via video link. "Eventually you feel trapped and alone, with nowhere to turn because you have never really submitted to church authority in your life. Your deceit turns upon you with the fullness of judgement that only you know. It's a tragic reality of rebellion. Nobody should be surprised when it turns out like this." He was intent on using Claire's death to draw conclusions that pointed towards obedience and submission to his authority. "Don't be overly concerned with this present sadness," he continued. "It will soon pass, and we will all be the better that this darkness has departed our ranks."

The service for Claire was brief and poorly attended. Her husband spoke quietly of the all too brief four years they had spent together and was entirely unconvincing in his statements of devotion towards her. The minister equally seemed uncomfortable and ill at ease in his praise of Claire's service to the church community in pastoral care, if genuinely remorseful that he had not been more available to Claire in her hour of need.

The rain was heavy as they loaded her casket into the back of the hearse and headed off with a few cars following into the traffic. Twelve thousand kilometres away, Hedgestone could not find sleep as his mind turned over, wondering what exactly had happened to Claire and what Jane Johnson was up to.

He felt an uneasiness at not being in control of the events before him. He knew something was on the move, but what exactly? He did not like this at all. He decided that with Claire gone and no one else on the ground to pursue Jane, that he would pause in his pursuit until he had intelligence of any further threats posed by her inquiries.

After Peter had farewelled the last guests of the wake held at his home, he silently wandered through the house. He paused in the bathroom and recounted the horror of finding Claire. The dramatic events of the last few days had had a two-fold impact upon him. He had not hated Claire. It was just that she was so much stronger than him, so much so that he felt compelled to find comfort in other places.

On the other hand, a new beginning was possible for him. He began to entertain all sorts of lies and possibilities. If Claire was the wife of his flesh, maybe he was now free to find the wife of his spirit? Such was the deceptive arguments Peter so often pondered when justifying the outcome of his motivation. He began to clean up the dishes left by the guests. As he unpacked the dishwasher, he picked up a carving knife and went to put it away in the knife block but noticed that there was no slot left. On taking a closer look at the knife, he realised it was not part of their kitchen knife set at all. Perhaps it belonged to the caterers who had bought food for the wake? Without further thought, he added Jane's knife to his drawer of odd kitchen utensils.

CHAPTER 30

GOING DEEPER

The shocking death of Claire and the events of the night before had left both Tommy and Jane in a state of speechless confusion.

Sorrow, regret and despair hung heavily over them. Claire was not the enemy. In many ways, she was just another victim of Hedgestone's destructive and domineering, life-controlling leadership. A willing participant in his regime — yes, absolutely. Motivated by her own gratifications — for sure.

Nonetheless, Claire had, at one time, chosen life and restoration over darkness and spiralling self-destruction. But in the midst of that quest, she had found in the church all of the same deceit and carnality she had encountered in the world that she had been desperate to leave behind. Perhaps she could have, like so many others, found the peace and second chance she so desired, but for Hedgestone, tapping and trapping her in a direction from which there was no way out.

Hedgestone had caused her to stumble, and he had no fear of consequential spiritual millstones around his neck — no fear of a God whose judgement might come one day looking for him. He was wholly given over to the self-deception that the ends justified the means, that his 'holy' cause came above the needs of others. Everyone was dispensable. One might call it a reprobate mindset — a seared conscious, a cold dead-heartedness that had long ago forgotten how to feel anything except hatred for that which threatened his control.

Jane and Tommy could not help but silently ponder that the very night they had submitted to a physical relationship, Claire had lost her life. While they were in the throes of deep intimacy, Claire was bleeding out in a bathtub.

This was not in the plan. Could they, should they, go to the police? Who would believe their story? Should they forget the whole Hedgestone thing? How many more lives could be jeopardised?

Days faded into weeks, with the severity of recent events weighing heavily on both of them. At times, they found themselves losing their confidence, both in themselves and in what they perceived as their righteous cause. Hedgestone was too powerful, too strong, too well-protected by layers of thick religious robes of self-righteousness and surrounded by circles of to-the-death loyal, faceless men that protected him from his crimes.

As a result, they found themselves in a paradoxical predicament. The events that had brought them together into a state of committed emotional closeness had also stunned and paralysed them, making it increasing difficult to make the decisions that needed to be made. They questioned their motives and their courage to resume the pursuit of their plan.

Hedgestone was a lot better at this then they could have imagined. The outcomes and vindications they had sought now seemed further away than ever before, mainly due to their own paralysis in pursuing them.

Worse still was that they began to distance themselves, not just from their cause, but from each other. It was the cause that had brought them together. As their shared purpose lost its hold on them, so they also felt their lives begin to drift apart.

All of this was distilling in Jane's mind, as she took a long run through the Botanic Gardens and past the Opera House. This was a route she loved taking at dusk — that magical period between peak hour traffic clearing and people coming out for dinner around Circular Quay in The Rocks precinct. She was always challenged by the beauty of the view from Mrs Macquarie's Chair, out across the harbour with the ferries making their way in both directions, their lights coming on as night fell.

In the distance, was the beautiful Harbour Bridge with its elegant structure spanning the waters in a confident strength, providing a connection so vital to the functioning of her city. Just before her was the Opera House, with its delicate sail-like structures, facilitating a meeting place for community and the exchanging of ideas and creativity through the performing arts. She always frowned when people described the Opera House as a venue for 'entertainment.' No, it was about a conscious and beneficial need for people to demonstrate and communicate much of what it means to be human, and to journey the often singular and lonely path of life. To love and to conquer, to fail and to win, to submit and to endure all of the challenges that life could set throw up, both kindly and harshly. There was a compelling need for humanity to share their stories, be it at the Opera House or on some prehistoric cave walls 10,000 years ago.

'Bridges and houses, places of gathering,' Jane thought. 'How appropriate that they sit side by side each other.' One spans the gap that enables people to come together at a nexus point where both ideas and encouragement for living a purposeful life could be exchanged.

Her heart drifted as it often did, to messages her father had shared with his congregation. Week to week, month to month, over many years, words that edified and built up a congregation, a community of faith, coming together to share life's challenges and create a house, a habitation of blessing and generational favour for so many families. It was all possible through the beautiful Bridge, the cross of sacrifice and love, in the blood shed to enable humanity to pass over a vast ocean of sin and failure that would seek to drown so many. The church as a gathering point of spiritual exchange, in whom her father so firmly believed, really was the hope for humanity, thought Jane.

Jane's thoughts continued to grow, one building upon another. Her father — what would he do in the circumstances that she and Tommy have just found themselves in? The first thing he would probably say was to stop sleeping together — and yeah, a pause right now might be a good idea. But more than that, he would point to the church, for which he had so dedicated and laid down his life. That needed to be rediscovered and recovered from the abuse suffered by the carnality of Hedgestone's style of leadership.

Finally, Jane began to feel that she was recovering her sense of bearing and direction. It was the church, the bride of Christ, those called out to join together in a single purpose, united by the message of the gospel, that was calling upon her to persist in taking down Hedgestone.

For just such a time as this, had she and Tommy come together in this endeavour. This was not her idea — something she had come up with. For the first time, she now realised that there had been a divine purpose at hand. 'This was something Jesus himself would want to be done,' thought Jane. It was his bride, his church, his Father's children that were being molested and spiritually murdered through Hedgestone's abuse.

Now encouragement began to replace despair as the stars above the harbour started to break through the midst of the darkness and cloud above her. The church deserved better leadership than this. The battle was no longer about her parents — this was spiritual warfare of the highest order. How could the world ever take the church and its message seriously with the behaviour of the Hedgestone kind? Not just within the humble ranks of believers, but in the very leadership of the church itself?

The church certainly had its work cut out for it in a rapidly changing world, with new generations emerging that were heavily under the influences of technology and wealth addiction, and a cultural departure from any sense of spirituality, a path that always ended in despair and a void of purpose. The church needed to be continuously repositioned and cleansed of carnal leadership abuse, just as it had been in previous generations as religiosity and ritual was left behind for the opening of the Word, for the *Just to live by Faith*, when Martin Luther got his hammer and nails out to make the point with his message on the door of a church in Wittenberg in 1517.

A sense of divine mission began to dawn upon Jane. She identified in herself many feelings and thoughts that she had recognised in her parents, and how they had lived and prioritised her life. There was a colour match of thought and motivation and purpose and idea. Once she recognised this in herself, she had a strange sense of being close to them, as if their legacy now lived within her — as if a banner and standard had been placed into her hands to carry forward.

Taking on Hedgestone was no longer a choice — it was an obligation, a determination of heart and spirit. She would pick up that banner from where she had dropped it in recent weeks and once again press onwards with the strategy already in place and within her reach. With Tommy by her side, this time she would not falter. Jane was urgent to share her newfound sense of purpose.

CHAPTER 31

PURPOSE IN PLANNING

Tommy was glad to hear of Jane's renewed commitment. In his mind, it was a good thing that their motivations and objectives had been tested by the unexpected and terrifying Claire event. They had less than two months before the Hedgestone global conference where they would execute their plan.

Tonight, they had arranged to get online with Paul in order to put the final touches to their plan and outline the crucial part that Paul would play in all of this, given his location stateside.

Tommy arrived at Jane's at about eight pm for the planning session. Jane quickly answered the door and ran back to her laptop, where she was already engaged with Paul in a Skype chat.

Tommy squeezed in alongside Jane. "Hi, Paul, sorry to interrupt your family time with Jane, how are you?"

"Hi Tommy, yes, all good here. Jane was just bringing me up to date on recent events. Wow, it sounds like this Claire was a crazy bitch; and Hedgestone, even crazier. This is all a lot more intense than what I thought. But I'm with you guys. Just let me know what you need me to do."

"Well, that's great. Let's get into it and refresh where we are up to. I know you were planning on trying to get to Sydney, but you are actually more valuable to us where you are right now. Jane has already registered as a freelance journalist with *Charisma*, a US evangelical church magazine. They have arranged for Jane, alias Mary-Anne Simkins, to do an interview with Hedgestone in between sessions at his up-and-coming conference in Arizona. The interview is booked for just before the evening international session where Hedgestone is set to preach to about 8,000 delegates in what is supposed to be the keynote event of the week's agenda. Now, here is what we need you to do. You have to get down to Arizona and join one of the local GOF churches."

Tommy paused, as he knew this was the first time Paul was hearing this.

"OK, well that's going to be interesting," Paul squeezed out with a very noticeable and uncomfortable hesitation.

Jane was silent. She had previously argued with Tommy about this part of the plan, explaining that she didn't want to put Paul in any danger, especially after the Claire incident.

"It's incredibly important that we have someone on the inside, Paul. You're the only one we can trust. Our research shows that they like to get new people into volunteering for service in the church as soon as they can. So, you need to get down there, ideally a month early, and join a GOF congregation — make some friends, play the newbie as best you can, and volunteer for sound desk ministry, given your experience in music production. They will be putting together a roster to run the sound and technical services desk for the conference. It's absolutely imperative that you get rostered on Thursday night, which is when Jane is booked for her green room 30-minute interview session with Hedgestone.

Jane will be wired for audio and video. At a strategic point in her interview, she will do a cutover of the transmission to an input you will control from the sound desk. Hedgestone has conference video screens set up all around the auditorium and throughout all the breakout rooms. The interview will then go unexpectedly live just as the delegates are taking their seats in the auditorium. They usually come early for the Thursday night session to get the best places. Remember, the end game is to get Hedgestone to be judged by his own 'peers.' So, we need to get in and get out, as quick as we can. Immediately following the cut to live, I've got all the digital media releases ready to roll out."

Again, Tommy paused to test for Paul's acceptance of the plan so far.

Paul was noticeably agitated. He had listened intently and politely without interrupting Tommy. A frown squeezed together by his raised eyebrows, together with a puzzled look in his eyes, was not a good sign.

"Guys, that's a lot for me to put together in a short time. You are relying on a lot of things falling into place that I might not be able to influence for you. I mean, there is a fair degree of random connections and positioning that will need to come together."

Jane decided it was time for her to offer some big sister support.

"Paul, that's all true, but we have time to reconfigure if you don't get on the roster for that night, but I'm sure you will. We've done a fair bit of research on how they work in Hedgestone's home territory. I know you will be fine. Remember, I will be in the green room doing the interview and I'm going to be relying on you getting the cutover in place and then protecting that sound desk from anyone who might try to intervene. Tommy will also be close by, ready to assist," assured Jane.

"Yeah, but how do I volunteer and get on this roster? And how do I manage the input from your device?" Paul asked, sincerely without wanting to shy away from the task being allocated to him.

Tommy was eager to put some perspective around these expected concerns.

"You won't need to influence them at all. These guys are extremely keen to get new people onto a roster and committed into the structure and command of their hierarchy. You just need to say the right things at the right time and connect with the sound team. You will be surprised at how quickly they will get you into place. Yes, getting on the Thursday night team might require some manoeuvring, but I've got some ideas on that once you get down there. I will send you the details on a Wi-Fi enabled USB device. You then just switch to that input from the sound desk. Remember, its audio and video."

Paul thought through Tommy's observations. "OK, well, let's get on with it. I mean what's the worst that could happen? They kick me out of church?"

Tommy and Jane stole a glance at each other, and were relieved that Paul had given a baseline commitment to the plan.

Jane then picked up the briefing with regards to logistics. They would send Paul some cash to fund any expenses he needed to get in place. They would meet him a week before for a dress rehearsal and dry run. After some final assurances, they signed off the Skype session with Paul.

Jane looked across at Tommy.

"You need to promise me you will keep Paul out of harm's way. If anything should happen to him, I don't know how I would handle it. He is all I have left," she said.

"Got it. I will be with Paul as soon as we cut over to live." They looked at each other for a moment. "Anyway, it's late. I should get going," Tommy said, breaking away from Jane's searching blue eyes.

Jane hesitated for a moment but then got up and walked Tommy to the door. "Sure, talk to you tomorrow. I will start working on travel arrangements."

Tommy and Jane had already had a chat about the night of the Claire attack and agreed to put the physical side of their relationship on hold until they got through the Hedgestone plan. They both realised that this would create some tension between them in the short term but would give them the chance to focus on their respective parts of the plan. Nonetheless, had either of them lingered a moment longer, they knew that that commitment could easily be renegotiated.

Ten days later, Jane had boarded QF11 bound for LA to execute on their plan. The significance and the possible impact of Project Monument, as they had named it, was not lost on her for a moment. As she settled in for the journey, she stole away from the present with her own thoughts, reciting to herself how she had come to be there.

People live lives that crisscross other people's lives. They come, they crisscross, they live, they love, they hate, they die. The randomness in timing and chance element of theit intersections always has the potential to create life moments that can set momentum and direction all anew, like billiard balls colliding into each other — impacting each other's path, like the breaking of a new set.

Two generations later, and nobody might really know or care that they lived. So often the question then becomes, why live at all? Does the striving for significance really bring about purpose? Are earthly births and departures just a boot camp to get to know the Creator through all the challenges of life's collisions with circumstances, people and events?

Jane pushed these thoughts around in her own mind as Tommy sat, already in his comfort zone in the seat next to her, headphones tightly fitted. Just three months ago, a letter from an old African preacher name Sipho had set the wheels of fate in motion, leading to a late-night phone call, followed by a trip to Africa, and then a death threat. And now here she was, on a plane to another continent to expose someone she had never met, who was responsible for the death of her parents, and accompanied by a man she had reconnected with and come to love and rely upon during the unfolding of these events.

'How does that happen?' Jane asked herself and anyone listening to her thoughts. She prayed a silent prayer, as she often did when her analytical mind hit a brick wall, 'God, you have to get involved here. It's your church. They're your people and even your leaders. This is your work.'

'Please,' she cried out in silent prayer, 'go before us. Protect us. Make way for your purpose and put an end to the abuse of your people. God, please, let those who have turned your house into a den of thieves, filling their own pockets, laying pretence and lie upon lie — let them be exposed for all to see. What they have done in the dark, let it be shouted from the rooftops.'

Jane felt she had now entered a silent flow of inspiration. The holy spirit within her began to fill her sails with wise and comforting words as the plane roared through the night sky. She wanted God's attention. Like Moses, she was determined not to go up to the challenge of redeeming God's purpose unless His presence went with her. Like the centurion whose daughter was near death, she put her confidence in His word and His presence to bring to life that part of her own life that had been taken away from her as a young and desperate 16-year-old girl. The reality and pain of that time was ample fuel to feed her claims before the throne of grace for many hours that night.

CHAPTER 32

MOMENT OF TRUTH

Some people find themselves thinking hateful thoughts, and the thought often goes something like this:

'I don't like you. It doesn't matter that I don't know you — I just don't like you. I don't like the colour of your skin, the shape of your body, the sound of your voice or the place you come from. I don't care about your job, your marriage or your family. You make me sick.'

These people who think these thoughts often use dehumanising phrases like *those kinds of people* and *people like them*. The value of the individual becomes lost in the subjection of a people group to a powerful and unrelenting prejudice — an unjustified hatred.

Arthur Hedgestone thought such thoughts, frequently and often. Blacks, Mexicans (or 'Blacksicans,' as he called them), native Americans — he didn't care. He was keen to be protected from having any association with those he considered 'other' at all. Jews and Asians fared little better. That the Jesus of his bible spoke words like 'Come to me *ALL* who are burdened,' did not include two-thirds of the non-European population on the planet, as far as his theology was concerned.

Would he let them come to church? Of course! He would take their money any day of the week, and not just on Sunday. Would he let them serve in music or car park ministry? Without a doubt, they could make up the church rosters. So long as he did not need to personally engage with them, touch them, minister to them, he would let them serve a purpose, which was really his purpose.

So when 'Mary-Anne Simpkins' of *Charisma* magazine emailed his personal assistant and requested an interview with him at his 45th International Bible Conference, complete with an inserted picture, he was more than receptive to the idea of spending some time with the young, blonde and blue-eyed journalist and even agreed to the special timeslot just before the keynote speech he was to give, provided the magazine agreed to the article being the promoted feature of the following monthly issue and also covered his principal address. Mary-Anne assured him her article would get front cover feature status, given the enormous regional influence of his movement across the southern bible belt of the US.

Jane arrived early for her six-thirty pm session with Hedgestone. She had spent the last three days locked up in a hotel room with Tommy, working on every nuance of her Mary-Anne Simkins persona, perfecting a southern US accent, complete with smiles and expressions lifted from watching endless hours of Trinity Broadcast Network tele-evangelists — not just her interview plan.

Tommy had been ruthless with her, emphasising the need to authentically capture and hold Hedgestone's interest in the interview. "Praise him," Tommy constantly drilled her. "He's an egomaniac. He thinks he is the fourth member of the Trinity. Feed the monster until he is within reach and then grab him by the throat and cut through."

When the time came, Jane presented herself at reception. "Hi, my name is Mary-Anne Simkins from *Charisma Publications*. I'm here to see Pastor Hedgestone."

The saccharine-sweet elderly lady behind the elaborate reception desk acknowledged Jane generously as if she had arrived for dinner. "Yes, of course you are, dear. Just take a seat for a moment, and I will let him know you have arrived."

As she found a space on the sofa, Jane tried to steel herself, bracing for the moment of truth. Tommy had confirmed that he and Paul were all in place. The auditorium was filling up fast with delegates, all focused on finding their seats for the seven-thirty preliminaries to the opening session from Hedgestone.

She did not have much more time to think as Mrs Honeysweet, the receptionist, was already back and beckoning Jane to follow her, leading her to a plush boardroom where she was pointed to a visitor's chair next to a small coffee table at the end of the room. Jane quickly positioned herself and checked that the wire she was wearing and the hidden camera she had brought, were correctly positioned and obscured from sight. Her heart was racing. She knew she needed 'Mary-Anne' to kick in real soon and take over.

Then it happened. Right there in front of her, Hedgestone entered the room.

"Well, hello, Mary-Anne," Hedgestone's voice boomed with an all-embracing, long lost friend confidence.

Jane could not admit to herself that she was intimidated by his presence. She silenced the voices within her, screaming to make a run for it. 'Greet him and get on with it,' she told herself.

Jane took Hedgestone's outstretched hand as Mary-Anne rose up in response to his greeting. "Pastor Hedgestone, it is such an honour and a privilege to meet you. Thank you so much for accepting my invitation."

"Not at all, not at all. Please take a seat Mary-Anne," replied Hedgestone as he took up the chair across from Jane.

Jane took out her notebook and attempted to present as 'journalistic' a facade as she could muster. "OK, I know you're due on the platform very shortly, so shall we start?"

"Of course, it's going to be a great night tonight. Have you seen the conference auditorium? I had eight 4 by 10-foot monitor screens installed all around the room just for this event. I hope you can stay for my message."

"Oh yes, I'm looking forward to that!" said Jane, smiling inwardly to herself and thinking how that could be interpreted in more ways than one.

"Now, how can I help?" asked Hedgestone, as he graciously tried to relax the room without relinquishing control.

"Pastor Hedgestone, this is your 45th annual conference, and it looks bigger than ever. The car park is overflowing. Can you tell us what you feel you contribute to the success and longevity of your ministry?"

"Faithfulness my dear, faithfulness. That's what the Lord is looking for."

Jane felt the first surge of anger rise within her. 'How dare he call me "dear!"'

She swallowed hard and continued to smile. "Looking back, do you think you have changed the way you do what you do, the way you reach people or run your ministries over time? Many churches these days seem to be endlessly pursuing 'relevance' and making sure they are young and contemporary in every sense and activity."

"I haven't changed a thing. God's given me a pattern that he hasn't given anyone else, and I'm not changing a thing."

"Do you think other churches and ministries have also been given a pattern?"

"I don't care what other churches are doing. Nobody else is doing what we are doing. Some try to copy us, but they usually fail miserably."

Jane decided it was time to up the tempo. "Some have charged your ministry with employing very controlling and at times threatening techniques — all in the name of discipleship. There are collectives of internet groups all posting exit stories, many of them quite horrific, saying their families were split upon instruction from you, that you practiced shunning and relational isolation, that you told them that they 'owe you their soul,' and that if they left the church, they would lose their salvation and go to hell. You make personal and unnatural regressive demands on people such as you not having a TV in the house. Or telling people that if they get caught going to the cinema, then they are disqualified for ministry. Or that the internet is a demonic strategy. Do you have any response to these allegations?"

Hedgestone was suddenly interested in the conversation but was no longer smiling.

"I make no apologies for our ministry style. If you don't like it, there are plenty of sloppy, faith lazy churches out there. Go find yourself one. We're not here to make people happy. We are here to make people holy. We are here to build the kingdom. If you are not a worker, then go find a lazy, happy go lucky, touchy-feely church. That's not us. We've got a job to do. We've got places to go, to the ends of the earth."

"What about compassion for the poor, ministries of assistance, the homeless, do these have a place in your pattern?"

"Jesus said the poor you will have with you always. They are not my problem. Get a job, Bob. I did. We don't do poverty."

Jane could feel Hedgestone's self-righteousness and pride rising with each answer. She felt he was well-positioned to launch the go-live. She reached for her hidden earpiece and clicked the trigger for Paul to plug and play. Paul was waiting, listening in to the whole conversation, received the notification and activated the live feed to the eight huge screens around the auditorium, which immediately flickered into life, with Hedgestone filling the entire screen and his voicing booming through the speakers. The delegates in the auditorium had mostly found their seats and immediately looked up with interest at the screens. This was great, they thought. They haven't done this before in previous years. Immediately they stopped to listen to their hero.

Tommy quickly moved into the sound room and told the guys they were wanted downstairs for a soundcheck on stage. As they left the sound room, Tommy entered after them and bolted the door, nodding to Paul to hold the vision and sound in place.

Jane continued. "Pastor Hedgestone, overseas church planting has been a long-term feature of your ministry."

"Yes it has, my dear. Yes, it has. 2,500 churches in 35 nations and I haven't finished yet!" Hedgestone was back in his favourite comfort zone, being given the opportunity to boast about his achievements. Jane felt she was on target, and approaching fast.

"And Africa seems to especially have been a focus for you?"

"Well, we seem to attract large numbers there. Those people don't know where they are going. They take to life leadership like honey to a bee."

"Pastor Hedgestone, do you remember a couple called the Johnsons, you sent to Mozambique in the 1970s, mostly at their own expense?"

Jane followed her question with an unrelenting stare, straight into the old man's squinty baby blue eyes. Hedgestone swallowed, drew breath and looked away for a moment.

"I, I don't recall that name," he stumbled out the lie.

"Let me help you," Jane coolly continued. She was just getting started. "Dale and Dominique Johnson, stationed in an urban area of Maputo, Mozambique. They died — shot dead, by car hijackers on the way back from a shopping trip to South Africa, by men that you hired, allegedly according to local testimony from one of the gang members."

All around the auditorium, the conference body began to check with each other, as the onscreen discussion lifted their interests.

"That's terrible. I never heard anything about that," Hedgestone lied. He was moving into his defensive zone — an unfamiliar place for him.

"Are you sure, Pastor Hedgestone? Because when somebody from your ministry dies in the field, I would have thought you might remember that? Do you remember any correspondence with Dale Johnson concerning African church finances being requested in order to remain in Africa and be used locally, rather than be sent back to your ministry in the USA?"

"Who are you?" Hedgestone squeezed out through gritted teeth.

Immediately, there was silence around the auditorium as everyone's attention became fixed to the screens.

Jane knew she didn't have long. She reached into her bag and pulled out a thick document.

"Pastor Hedgestone, this is a sworn statement by one of the hijackers who pulled the trigger that day. He testifies that the hit was requested by American pastors from your ministry."

Jane continued quickly. "And here is a fully detailed chronology of email and letter correspondence in relation to Dale Johnston being threatened by you, forcing him to resign his ministry or hand over money to your ministry in the US. Pastor Hedgestone, do you make it a habit of taking money from poor and needy African churches?"

"I know who you are! You're that bitch daughter of the Johnson's causing me trouble in Australia!"

Gasps and horrific looks did the Mexican wave around the auditorium. They had never heard Hedgestone speak like this, let alone the facts that were being presented.

"Pastor Hedgestone, here is a copy of contracts and payments and bank transfers that demonstrate without a doubt that you are skimming the expenses of several churches by charging management fees via a series of tax-exempt entities that end up in personal accounts controlled by you here in the US."

Hedgestone was a trembling, jelly angry mess by now. His lips quivered. His hands shook. His voice lost its authority but not its anger.

"You get out! Get out now! You can never prove any of this! Johnson was a trouble maker. He threatened to undo all of our work in Africa. He had to be stopped. He was supposed to be scared, not killed."

"But you failed to tell your bully boys in Africa that, didn't you?"

Hedgestone was on his feet.

"Pastor, if that is what you should be called, how much, and how long have you been stealing from God's people? How many people have you killed along the way? Pastor, do you believe in eternal judgement, that judgement should start in the house of God? Because these people do!"

With that, Jane had walked over to the screen in the room and flicked on the TV monitor of the feed to the auditorium. The monitor showed the stunned congregation in the auditorium, peering up at the screen, shocked and speechless; some in tears, others consoling each other.

"They are waiting for you, Pastor. What will you preach to them tonight? More sacrifice? More giving? How about repentance? *Thou art the man!* Maybe mercy? Because you are going to need it!"

Hedgestone fell backwards into his chair, shaking, as many of his assistants and aids rushed from the auditorium into his office.

Jane was not quite done. "You killed my parents. You robbed us of our lives. I hope to see you rot in prison. You will have plenty of time to read your bible and write your sermons there."

The crescendo of judgment was rising in Jane's voice. She was amazed no one had yet asked her to leave.

"Your movement has become nothing more than a monument. A monument to your own pride and self-indulgence. You were given so much, and if it wasn't enough, you would have been given even more. You were told to use the gold but not touch the glory, but you wanted the glory for yourself, as well as the gold. Once there was a purpose, but you made yourself and your dynasty the purpose. You enthroned yourself and kicked God off his own throne. You're in love with the sound of your own voice — you are not even listening for God's. You are not a pilgrim; you are a proprietor. You are not on a pioneering journey; you want to own everything you touch. How can you justify what you've done?"

It was over for Hedgestone as he gazed up at the monitor into the faces of his delegates. "I preach the gospel," he muttered.

"Yeah, but you don't live it. It's not who you are. It's just a profession to build yourself an empire. An empire that you control without accountability — where the end justifies the means. You like to sound so righteous, but you are no different to the Pharisee's of Jesus' day — the whitewashed tombs that loved the religious gowns and outward appearances and traditions, lauding it over as many as they could, while inside they were nothing more than filthy dead man's bones. They could not enter the kingdom of God themselves and stopped others entering in. *Thou art the man,* Hedgestone!"

Jane stormed out through the auditorium, shaking, tears beginning to well up in her eyes. 'It's done. It's over….'

She looked ahead into the crowd. Thousands of people, many petrified like pillars of stone, as white as ghosts; others, angry and shaking fists; others still, in total confusion and disarray, shaking their heads. Where was her Tommy? Where was Paul? She looked up at the sound room.

Tommy and Paul were not finished. They switched the feed to their tag. The screens now detailed:

*For a full account of this interview and the illegal activities of Gospel Fellowship Ministries under the leadership of Arthur Hedgestone, please go to **www.themonument.net.au.***

People were reaching for the phones to hit the website where all of the substantiation, evidence and copies of documents had been uploaded and were instantly available for download.

Inside the sound room, Tommy and Paul where high-fiving each other, looking out at the auditorium below them in complete disarray, oblivious to the banging on the door and the requests to 'open the door, or we will call the police.'

Tommy looked at Paul. "Time to go home," he said.

"Can you believe my sister? She left nothing on the field, took no prisoners, showed no mercy," Paul observed with a fair degree of pride in his sibling.

"Yep, I can believe it. I never doubted her for a moment. Let's see if we can find her and get out of here," said Tommy. He quickly texted Jane to meet at the agreed pickup point. He opened the door to a hoard of confused techies,

"Guys the room is all yours, but if I were you, I'd be looking for another gig. This one is over," he said and pushed his way through them.

Jane heard her phone buzz and remembered they were to meet where Tommy's rental was parked. Her head was spinning. 'Wow! Did that just happen?'

She continued to push her way through the crowd. All around her, confusion reigned. This conference meeting was not going to start on time, if at all! She saw what appeared to be GOF leaders in huddles with arms folded, deep in serious discussion. Then as she walked on, something very strange happened. The whole room went into a dizzy slow motion. She saw first-hand the raw damage and the avalanche of hurt that had come down on so many ordinary, well-intentioned, God-fearing and serving men and women, families, young people, old people. Jane looked into their faces. Shock, betrayal, tears and fears filled their faces.

Compassion rose up in her heart for them, but she knew there was only one way out for them as there was for her. She was feeling within her what they must feel at this very moment. She felt that same absence of spirit she'd felt that day not so long ago when all of this had started. The day she stood in the midst of a regular Sunday service congregation, feeling strangely disconnected, as if she was invisible — an intruder into the joy of others — not permitted to participate or partake in their collective experience. Perhaps, in part, by her own volition. It was that same intense aloneness that seemed to have fallen on all those around her. She had conquered that spirit, but their battle still lay before them and was just beginning.

A sense of urgency now began to overtake her. How could she help them? She needed to talk to Tommy quickly. Finally, she made her way out to the carpark and saw the boys standing by the rental, looking intensely for her.

"Paul, Tommy!" she called out to them, breaking into a run in their direction. They heard and saw her. Falling upon each other, the three of them embraced. They knew it was finished. The impact they had achieved would now take its own course and do what work still needed to be done.

CHAPTER 33

HOME

Tommy's hire car sped off into the night for the airport. The plan was for all three of them to fly back to Sydney that same night and not hang about for any inquiries or respond to any reactions. All of that would be done from Australia. They would not go looking for it, or let any fallout find them. Their job was done. Hedgestone was exposed and tried before his own fraternity and fellowship. This was their mess to clean up now.

"Jane, you were amazing!" Tommy said as soon as they were on the highway. "We had goosebumps crawling all over both of us. Even we believed it was 'Mary-Anne Simkins' and not Jane Johnson in that green room."

"I just knew I only had one chance at this. I had to execute exactly as we planned – every word, every phrase, every motion. This was your work, Tommy. And Paul, you owned that sound room!" said Jane, reaching out to embrace her brother yet again. "You know what this means, don't you, Paul? I believe we can live again the life our parents intended us to live. We don't need this distance between us anymore. It's over. It's dealt with."

Jane found herself again unable to hold back tears.

Paul looked at the big sister he had so relied upon and looked to for security when growing up. "I'm so sorry Jane, for all those years we wasted, living in a relational wilderness because the hurt of being in your presence was more than I could bear – too many painful memories. I thought being alone would heal, but it didn't.

The scars just got deeper. I get that now. Don't worry, I'm with you – whatever our next is, I'm going to be in it!"

Tommy was overjoyed with what he heard as he drove on. This was more than he had hoped for.

It wasn't long before they had checked in at the airport and were settling into the departure lounge. Paul had gone off to get coffees, leaving Tommy and Jane alone.

"Well, that was a buzz, Jane," said Tommy trying to get their feet back on the ground.

Jane just reached out her hand and grabbed Tommy's and nodded silently with an awesome smile and quiet satisfaction filling her eyes. Their moment was interrupted when Paul returned with a tray of coffees and, looking up at the TV monitor in the lounge, called out to them, "Hey, look at this!"

They turned their attention to the screen and saw a CNN reporter standing outside the GOF headquarters in Phoenix, Arizona.

"…I'm coming to you live from outside the headqu*arters of* the Gospel Outreach Fellowship church where their annual global conference was due to kick off tonight, with over 8,000 said to be in attendance from over thirty countries. Apparently, a live cross to an interview with the GOF leader, Arthur Hedgestone and a Mary-Anne Simkins from Charisma magazine was force-fed into the auditorium, and is said to have shown Hedgestone confess to involvement in the death of some of his missionary workers almost 15 years ago. As well as that, documents alleging major financial impropriety were put before him and are now freely available from a website, www.themonument.net.au. We'll bring you more once we find out what's going on here. Right now, it's a scene of massive confusion and lots of hurt people finally making their way out and I imagine going home…"

The three of them just looked at each other. Finally, Tommy shrugged his shoulders and said, "Well, that happened quicker than I thought."

In the distance, the boarding call for their flight was breaking through their collective amazement. They were so looking forward to getting home.

Before they landed back in Sydney, Hedgestone had been forced by his puppet board of elders to resign, effective immediately. But that had made no difference. Hundreds of churches announced their separation and disassociation with GOF, who declared their intention to function independently. Hedgestone's movement was over.

The FBI was rumoured to be opening an investigation into the global financials of Hedgestone and his organisation, as well as the circumstances surrounding the death of Dale and Dominique Johnson. The secular morning breakfast shows, as well as Christian cable TV were all running talk fests, dissecting the GOF scandal and questioning how the authority that had led to the abuse had managed to run so deep for so long. Many former GOF members were coming forward and giving testimony about their experience with Hedgestone and his horrendously oppressive, relational intimidation, including the aggressive shunning tactics he employed to divide and silence any critics.

While Tommy and Jane had no intention of becoming media targets, they knew it was only a matter of time before they would be located. Jane already had Tommy working on the dedicated Monument website to add some pages for self-help for those who found themselves feeling bewildered and betrayed by Hedgepoint's deception and abuse of their faithfulness and loyalty to GOF.

However, there was a more pressing new project that required their attention. Jane and Tommy had a wedding to plan…

CHAPTER 34

UNITED

Bellbird Hill in the Blue Mountains won out as the wedding venue over the Harbour Bridge precinct – not that Tommy really had any involvement in the location or venue determination. Tommy and Jane had agreed on simplicity and a minimal guest list. They also both wanted Sipho Mbane there, and despite some visa challenges, he made it onto the front row of well-wishers before them.

It was six weeks since they had returned from the USA. And four months since this had all begun, when, in the midst of a church service, Jane's spirit had experienced a frightening and violating displacement.

Now, in an entirely different spirit of service, they stood on a hill, facing each other, hand in hand, with a local pastor friend of theirs running proceedings. Jane closed her eyes for a split second and subconsciously compared the two moments, taking a break from the present to absorb and process the arrival of happiness, of entering into the light from a dark and confused place. A gorgeous green valley fell away behind the minister while their friends and family gathered in front of them with the golden afternoon sun shining on the celebration of their union.

Their vows were exchanged with all the sincerity one could expect from the deep love that Jane and Tommy had found in each other through the sequence of events that had unfolded over the last four months. But the words of their vows were subordinate to the lock Jane and Tommy's eyes had on each other. They gazed deep into each other's souls and were joined that day, not just by spoken covenants but with all the intensity of the honesty and integrity of that look of love. As they spoke the words, their eyes never lifted from each other.

Finally, they blinked as their lips joined before the minister could complete the words, "You may kiss the bride." After prolonged cheers, they released each other and acknowledged the goodwill of their 120 guests. They both turned to look into the late afternoon sun and soaked up the warmth of its presence.

Jane pulled Tommy close and whispered in his ear, "Do you remember watching the glorious African sunsets together when we were just kids?"

"They were surely glorious, colourful and enjoyably slow in the going down, but this one beats them all!" He embraced his fully surrendered bride again.

Jane closed her eyes and just for a moment, felt deep within her spirit a moment of grief that her parents were not with her on this important day. She imagined them as she remembered them – in their prime of life, holding hands as they so often did, and sensed without a shadow of a doubt, their pleasure about her and Tommy. Instantly, any lingering grief evaporated from her as an ocean of happiness and joy swept over her and raised her spirit to a new level.

Again, Jane found Tommy's dark eyes, "C'mon, let's go find ourselves a new adventure."

She grabbed Tommy's hand firmly in her own and walked through the crowd towards the awaiting limousine. Her bridesmaids help fold her lace and satin dress into the car. Tommy closed the car door behind her, farewelled the guests and joined Jane in the back seat. As the car pulled away from the crowd, the sun rays broke through the rear window. He took Jane's face gently in his hands, kissed her softly for a moment. Finally, their future belonged to each other.

THE END